For my dad.

This is a work of fiction. The names, characters, businesses, places, events, locales, and incidents are the products of the author's imagination or used in a fictitious manner. Any resemblance to actual persons, living or dead, or actual events is entirely coincidental.

http://lucidfitzpatrick.com

Fitzpatrick, Lucid.
The Fall Line: a novella / Lucid Fitzpatrick
ISBN 979-8-9908357-0-2
FIRST EDITION
Publication Date: October 1, 2024

First published in the United States of America by Lucid Fitzpatrick.

THE FALL LINE

CONTENTS

Part One: *The Alpenglow*

A SKIER HOLDS NO ENVY TOWARD A BIRD SOARING IN THE SKY.

Zack Reeves caught sight of a golden eagle from the snowy mountain peak. The heavy storm front shifted in blooming maneuvers against the crosswinds, but the eagle hovered in a fixed point, flexing its courage beneath the battalion of threatening—but idle—winter clouds. The snowstorm offered its first reprieve after barraging the mountain for two weeks, and Reeves watched the bird with a naked eye as it perched in front of a veiled Sun, held captive behind the gray shroud. The still frame exploded into action as the starving eagle tucked its wings and dived into a free fall to catch its first meal since the storm began. Reeves stood alone on the mountaintop and watched the streaking bird disappear into a distant valley. Swirling dust fell from the sky, and Reeves smiled at the winter covenant, happily accepting a diving eagle and fresh flurry in place of a docile dove and broken olive branch.

White ash covered the frozen landscape under the gray skies. The storm brought a season's worth of snow in a fortnight, leaving The Seraphs Ski Haven drawn in grayscale over a white canvas and begging to be filled with the color of daring skiers. Reeves was an abstraction of the setting as if he were mined of its raw ore. Dashes of gray hair capped his tall frame like a fresh snowfall, and the scruff grown over the planes of his jaw matched the cold cloud cover. The hint of his blue eyes brought the first color to the scene, magnified by his jacket, which glowed with the blue of an exposed glacier. The light snow covered the tops of his skis, which soon disappeared under the accumulation. Reeves presided over a pristine snow cover that left the slope as smooth as a still pond in the early morning. A quiet laugh dispelled the thoughts passing in Reeves' mind. "What a shame to disturb this perfect serenity," he said in silence, "and what audacity to take it for myself." Just as a sculptor seeks a perfect slab to carve, Reeves tucked his elbows into his ribcage and dived into his own free fall down the top section of The Second Seraph.

The muted sun crowned the four peaks of The Seraphs Ski Haven, breathing light into the quiet valley below. Angular shadows cut the village buildings in half, leaving the illusion of a town bowing in homage to the morning coronation. The steep slopes evaded the morning light, leaving the freshly groomed snow with its natural cold-blue luminance. Indeed, the ski resort held the allure of royalty: in nobility, tempting the ambitious with promises of glory; and in warning, deterring the timid amidst its danger. The Seraphs was a skier's mountain where professionals trained for the highest competition and the most advanced amateurs sought to prove their merit. And just as animals migrate in search of fertile and flourishing grounds, the winter calls skiers to the mountain.

A string of gondolas climbed to the summit as a soft wind wisped across the terrain below, stirring the fresh dust on the virgin slope. The snow swirled in the shape of a living smoke and danced like a ritual of incense blessing the mountain.

Excitement exceeded expectation for the first group of passholders as their gondola passed the mountain's midpoint. Chatter filled their carriage as the skiers discovered the surreality of being the target of their own envy; the group coveted what was to come. They pointed in marvel over the mountain's beauty, the unblemished runs, and the prospect of being the first to carve into the slopes. As they rose, their sense of custody over the mountain grew. The words "first tracks" repeated among the group as if they were the artist's signature on the mountain's canvas. Their gaze fixed on the mountain, and one by one, the skiers fell silent upon the sight of a man in a bright blue coat sweeping down the hill.

Gasps filled the space left by the group's stunned silence as they watched the lone skier command the steep slope. The skier held a tight form; his boots, knees, and hips moved as a singularity, and his skis held together as if riding a single plank. Only the motion in his wrists seemed conscious, leading the skier's path. His line exposed the native resonance of the slope, bounding through arced turns at constant intervals, never wavering from the mountain's natural tempo. Speed gave him fluidity, and his technique looked so effortless that he transformed skiing into a carefully choreographed dance. The group in the gondola watched in awe until the skier disappeared over a ridge behind them. They surrendered any thoughts of dominion over the mountain as they admired the trail left by the skier —a single line drawn as a symmetrical wave etched into the snow.

At the bottom of the run, red letters spelled "Salt Mine Express" across the white panels that covered the lift engines. Below the sign, a lift operator raised a broom and quickly swept a collection of white powder off of a bench. Three young men sat on the clean seat, and the operator sent them up the slopes. As the operator turned to inspect the next chair, he saw the man in the blue coat dropping down the ridge toward his lift. He stuck the bottom of the broomstick on the ground, wrapped his arms around the snow-covered bristles, and watched the skier complete the run. The skier's style reached an aesthetique that betrayed anonymity. The lift operator need not see the skier's face nor the name on his ski pass. If an artist's work reveals his soul, then Zack Reeves skied as a naked spirit. Reeves made a sharp turn near the base of the lift line. His momentum carried him through the lane, stopping short of the loading zone.

"Look at that! Preacher-man gets first tracks this morning," the lift operator said in a youthful voice, referencing—in error—Reeves' nickname on the mountain. Reeves ignored the comment altogether. "I just got cleared to load riders on my lift. How'd you get up the mountain to make first tracks so early?" the lift operator asked.

"Caught a lift on a snow cat. I'm friendly with a driver," Reeves said in a venerable voice, weighed by years of breathing cold, dense air.

"No lesson today? Is that why you're out here by yourself?"

"I haven't had a client in over a week. This storm blocked the tourist flow. Too few are brave enough to drive up Cottonfalls Pass. It's all for the best, though. The snow has been too good this week. I woke up today with an urge to ski alone."

"You should always ski with a partner."

"Solitude suits me better," Reeves said, closing his eyes with a shrug. He dropped the words as a sandbag, blocking a current of emotion. The word partner tripped a subconscious reflex, bringing an immediate image to the front of his mind—a picture of warm cheeks inside the frame of strawberry blonde hair. His eyes closed to draw the image into focus; the shrug was an attempt to dismiss it.

"How is it out there? As good as advertised?" the operator asked.

"Glorious. I've gone entire seasons without having a run like that first lap."

"You can't beat the honor of making first tracks."

"How am I first tracks with those kids riding up there?" Reeves said, pointing his pole at the occupied chair climbing up the mountain.

"They got here same as you. Bribed a cat driver. Got here half-an-hour ago and just waited for my lift to open. The only tracks on the mountain right now are yours, Preacher."

"It's *Brother*," Reeves said, correcting the operator and wincing over both the mistaken and corrected alias.

"Oh, is it? I knew it was something old and religious."

"I'm not old. Or religious," Reeves said, pressing and turning his right foot.

"Aren't you, though? I've heard you yelling at your clients, teaching that old style like you're some kind of evangelist. Just look at those long, stiff breadsticks you're still using," the operator said, tapping the end of his broomstick on the tip of Reeves' ski. "They're so clumsy. You won't find any racer or free skier on this rock who uses skis like that anymore. I don't know how you do it on those behemoths. You may have the prettiest skiing on the mountain, but there's a reason that none of the pros here look like you, *Brother*."

"The shortest distance between two points is a straight line, but no one admires a stick figure," Reeves said with an honesty that responded to the words, forgetting for a moment that he spoke them aloud and to another person.

"What the hell does that mean?"

"Forget it," Reeves said, still checking his equipment. "Got a Phillips-head in there?" Reeves asked as he removed his ski and pointed to the operator booth.

The lift operator tossed the broom aside, reached into the booth, and handed the tool to Reeves. Reeves slipped out his gloves, pushed the head of the tool into his toe piece, and made a micro-turn, adjusting the binding on his right ski. He handed the screwdriver back to the lift operator and re-mounted his ski.

"That's it?" The lift operator asked.

"Binding felt loose."

"You didn't even tighten it. That can't have made a difference."

"Like I said, it felt loose," Reeves said, satisfied after a quick test of the adjustment.

"You are a monk," the operator said.

"That's what they say."

"They also say you've spent your whole life chasing the perfect run. With these conditions, today might be the day to catch it. I heard the forecast is so good, the national team extended their training here for another week."

"Thanks for the screwdriver," Reeves said, ignoring the lift operator's comments about his reputation.

"Enjoy your day off, *Brother*," the lift operator said. He grabbed his broom and swept off the next chair for Reeves. Reeves nodded and entered the loading zone.

The chairlift bounced before it steadied itself on the express cable, driving toward the peak of The Second Seraph. The ground descended as the chair fell towards the sky. The cold air scraped over Reeve's exposed cheeks, and his stomach sank to his waist while he rose higher up the mountain. His back and neck tightened, but no matter how taut he kept his body, he felt dizzy, as if his conscious was disoriented and disconnected from his body. Reeves gripped the safety rail across his lap and took a deep breath, feeling his legs dangle between the weight of his skis and the weightless sensation of being suspended in the air. A slow, condensed fog left Reeves' pursed lips as he released an intentional exhale and leaned over the side of the chair—beyond its safety. He focused on the base of the trees as he forced himself to look down to face his fear of heights—just as he did every time he got on a lift. Reeves knew stories of people conquering their fears, but in forty years of skiing—and thousands of chairlift rides—overcoming his acrophobia proved a futile hope.

Without warning, the lift stopped mid-ride with a soft jolt, leaving Reeves to dangle four stories above the steep slope. The chair bounced with the shifting tension of the line, and Reeves remembered that skiers spend most of their time on the mountain riding the lifts. He stared at the slope below, eyes drawn in contemplation as if to question why he subjected himself to such torture. After a moment, Reeves found a waving trail traced in the mountainside. Broad strokes widened the contours of the trail's tight curves, while thin, ruthless lines threaded the arcs together with proportions that transformed the remnant tracks into elegant calligraphy. Reeves had his answer.

The lift resumed. By the halfway point, Reeves settled into the ride and surveyed the conditions, noting which runs would be skied early and which he should hit first—a plan formed in Reeves' mind. "Start with the backside of The First Seraph," he thought, "before the crowds build. The snow is great there; it will be the best skiing of the day. Then, shift over to the bottom half of The First Seraph for the rest of the morning since the tourists will be busy exploring the top of the mountain. Grab lunch at the base lodge, then cover The Fourth Seraph, and hit the rest of the mountain as I make my way back." Reeves was happy with his plan but remembered what the lift operator told him—the national team extended their stay. "So avoid The Second Seraph," he concluded, "half of the front side will be blocked for training and the other half will be obstructed with curious observers."

Up ahead, the three young men bounced carelessly on their chair. Even from a distance, Reeves could see their recklessness. On the right edge, one of the young men danced with his hands in the air while another knocked his dangling skis together, ridding them of their collected snow. Reeves heard the clapping skis and watched the mix of slush and ice drop to the ground. The height of the fall gave the illusion of slow motion, only revealing the extent of the plummet at the moment of impact. Above the large crater where the icy debris crashed, the skier in the middle seat pointed at the V-shaped horizon where the Second and Third Seraphs converged. The young man who danced gave him a playful shove as he pointed. Their mischief left the chair swinging like a pendulum, closing within an arm's length of a passing lift tower.

Reeves' eye clung to the ridge in the distance

where the young man had pointed, and his concern reached a fever pitch. He forgot their reckless behavior, the swinging chair, and the falling snow. In fact, Reeves forgot about the height altogether. He only thought of Two-and-a-Half Pass, the passage between the Second and Third Seraphs, the tree-ridden path to the backside of the mountain known as Hallow's Gallows, and beyond that, *The Falls*.

The Falls was a legendary run without a legend. The skiing community was filled with third and fourth-hand accounts of men who claimed to have successfully skied the off-limits territory on the back side of The Seraphs. There was no evidence, no witnesses, nor any first-hand accounts. *The Falls* were part of Semitry National Park, a federally-owned and protected wildlife preservation adjacent to The Seraphs. Reeves heard its legends growing up, and when he joined The Seraph's ski school, he learned directly of the inevitable peril for anyone who dared ski *The Falls*. Once or twice a season, alerts sound over a missing skier. It wouldn't be until the late spring, when the base of the mountain thawed, that a Semitry ranger would find a frozen corpse adorned with mangled ski gear. Surviving The Falls was an impossibility. Successfully skiing it would constitute a miracle. And Reeves was not a religious man.

They're smarter than they let on, Reeves thought to himself as he watched the young men. He continued: It's too early to expect skiers from the base to reach this part of the mountain. I doubt ski patrol expects anyone near *The Falls* this early.

Reeves pulled a hand radio from his blue jacket and tuned it to the mountain's emergency channel.

"This is Zack Reeves. I'm riding up Salt Mine and eye-balling a group of bogies who might be fixing to run *The Falls*. Anyone patrolling near Two-and-a-Half Pass? Over," Reeves said into the handset.

"Zack, this is mountain dispatch. That's a negative on any patrollers nearby. Over."

"Hey, Zack, this is Jerison," another voice chimed on the radio. "What's their ETA? Pac and I are patrolling this morning, and we're just about to unload from the gondola at Head Lamp. We can sprint over to Two-and-a-Half in about twenty. Over."

"Twenty minutes will be five too late if these jokers head there," Zack replied. "I'll speed over and cut them off before they drop in. Over."

"Roger. If they try, stall the idiots until we get there to escort them off the mountain. Any idea how they get up there so early? Over."

"Caught a ride on a snowcat. Got dropped off at the bottom of Salt Mine. Figure out who the driver was and tell him he owes us a round tonight. Over."

"Roger that. Shouldn't be hard to I.D. their passes when they scanned in on Salt Mine. See you over by Hallow's Gallows, *Brother*. Over and out."

"Over and out."

The three young men slid off at the top of the lift. Reeves watched as they situated their gear and surveyed the empty mountain. Each skier in the group mounted a large backpack and aimed their skis toward The Third Seraph and Hallow's Gallows. Reeves recognized the signs: straps on their packs to hold their skis; the equipment needed to hike through Hallow's Gallows; and a hope to hike out of Semitry National Park. Casual passholders do not carry such gear—any doubt of their intention burned away from Reeves' mind. The young men's intention was clear.

The remaining moments of the chairlift ride stretched out before him. Still, Reeves sat back in the chair, calmed by the quiet hum and vibration from the lift. He relaxed more with each turn of the bullwheel. Stopping the foolish skiers would be a simple task. The moment's urgency diminished; Reeves felt no rush to chase the kids as he counted his advantages. The mountain was his backyard. He knew every run, pass, and path. He surmised that the young men would not know the precise point to enter Hallow's Gallows and access The Falls. Reeves knew. He also knew that, no matter their skill, he could best their speed.

A soft draft blew over the mountain, gently pushing the chair and whispering soft static across Reeves' ears. The cool air felt refreshing, and the sound of soothing static meshed with the sway of the chair as it caught the wind. It was enough to put any man to sleep. Reeves was shocked when he reached the sign that read "Ski Tips Up." He shoved off the chair and cruised down the ramp and onto Dark Adits, the sprawling run below Salt Mine Express. Reeves skimmed over the snow, pulled his gloves over his hands, and lowered his goggles without breaking his motion. He coasted down the mild slope, almost adrift save the ski tips that pointed like an arrow at Dark Adits … to Mine Bender … across Railcart catwalk … then down Denominator … to Two-and-a-Half Pass … and, finally, Hallow's Gallows.

How can any man be so reckless as to gamble against the expense of his own life? There's no reward granted under certain death. Reeves examined these thoughts as he built speed over Dark Adits. He knew men acted impulsively and compulsively, especially young men seeking immediate gratification without regard for long-deferred consequences. He thought of those who drank, and smoked, and chased women to excess. Even the hardest bender would leave breath in a man's lungs, he thought, but running The Falls is an act that exceeds innocent, victimless debauchery. Reeves noted that The Falls never inspired casual curiosity and invariably provoked a morbid obsession leading to blasphemy—not against any god or religion—but against one's own life.

Reeves' skis lost the slope as his speed sent him airborne over a ridge. The snap of the skis sent an echo over the empty slope when he landed. Reeves passed the triumphal archway that presided over the eastward side of the run and adorned a set starting gates for the racecourse. The ridge was the official beginning of Mine Bender, the steepest and longest run on all of The Seraphs, running over three thousand vertical feet down The Second Seraph. Lines of blue dye ran along the western half of the slope, beginning at the archway's starting gate and stretching beyond a racer's vision. Reeves hugged the slope's western edge, respecting the area reserved for the national team's training.

He muted his speed as he traversed the racing trail. He knew catching Railcart catwalk required a hard stop mid-run on Mine Bender. The catwalk had just enough room for two skiers to run side-by-side and wrapped around to the backside of the mountain in a tight, uphill curve. If he carried too much speed, he'd miss it—or worse, end up crashing into the thicket of aspen trees below the narrow path. Reeves measured his approach to the catwalk, trying to preserve some momentum into the cramped trail. He pressed the edges of his skis hard into the slope, but the bend proved too tight. Reeves came to a standstill just below the catwalk's opening. He stepped to pivot his skis and complete the hairpin turn. Tracks from the three young men littered the catwalk floor. Reeves saw them and dug the sides of his skis into the snow, pushing one leg after the other and shoving his poles into the trail as he skated in pursuit.

The skate across Railcart dropped skiers onto Denominator, a long, twisting path through the backside forest of The Second Seraph. Denominator's length nearly matched Mine Bender, but officials deemed it unsafe for racing due to the danger of the trees aligning the narrow run.

Denominator's trail line swung Reeves back and forth like a swerving pendulum. His motion transformed from effortless to helpless, leaving him hypnotized by his own action. Reeves could not tell if he took a moment for himself or if the moment took him over. Regardless, he forgot his immediate mission in the joy brought by his favorite run on the mountain. The trail was not a memory but a permanent pathway seared in his mind. Reeves navigated on nostalgia. The path opened before him like a cherished childhood song where melody and lyrics manifest without anticipation or thought. Patterns among the trees and the sensation in his feet as his skis scraped the snow were subconscious cues that kept Reeves making turns in time with the trail's natural rhythm. Coil followed recoil as Reeves sank his knees deep into the peak of each turn, only to shoot upright as if shocked by the energy of the mountain. His bright blue jacket bounced along Denominator's contours like a motor piston thrusting inside an engine block, ignited by the slope and combustion of speed.

A shallow crater scooped the earth from the flat mountain step where Denominator ceded to Two-and-a-Half Pass. Reeves cut across the bowl's edge, hugging the rim to short-cut a route to the front lines of Hallow's Gallows. The curved slope's centripetal force tested the elasticity of his skis, but Reeves pressed underfoot to keep contact with the snow. He swooped to the head of Hallow's Gallows and stepped out of his bindings in a single motion.

The three young skiers stood near the center of the bowl, orienting themselves on the mountain and trying to determine a path to *The Falls*. The trio stood in a line facing the impenetrable curtain of trees that stood like a blockade protecting the backside of the mountain. The weight of their skis —now mounted on their packs—forced each of the skiers into a slight hunch as they scouted the terrain. One of the young men braced against his poles, while his eyes failed to penetrate the dense forest. The two others huddled over a trail map, a phone, and a compass, searching for direction. Preoccupied with their dislocation, they did not notice Reeves emerge from Denominator. The pair looking at the map looked up and pointed toward the treeline just beyond where Reeves stopped. Reeves watched the three young men pack their devices and begin a slow, awkward walk, rocking heel-to-toe with ankles locked inside their ski boots, to the far end of Hallow's Gallows.

Reeves hoped that his presence alone would be

enough to dissuade them from their suicidal gambit. Hope proved futile; the three young men continued to trek towards the trees. Reeves marched to cut them off. He noted the young men's formidable, calculating purpose. Their procession toward The Falls was devoid of apprehension, like a group of gamblers approaching a casino table with an untested strategy but novel advantage play. Reeves moved to intercept them, knowing they miscalculated their odds.

They ignored Reeves, even as he trudged toward them, plodding through the snow in his ski boots. As he got closer, Reeves was surprised at the young men's demeanor. There was no sign of the playful recklessness they displayed on the chairlift. Their eyes were sharp in concentration and completely conscious of what they were doing. Physics teaches that energy cannot be created or destroyed, only transformed. The nervous energy of anticipation the trio displayed on the chairlift was gone. In its place, the young men harnessed the focused energy of execution.

Reeves noticed more details in their equipment. Each of them outfitted their pack with an avalanche airbag, and Reeves recognized a yellow radio dangling on a lanyard around one of the skier's necks—an avalanche transceiver. They were thoughtful and prepared. Moreover, Reeves did not see any cameras or mounts on their helmets or in their packs, nor did they stop to record commentary or document their escapade. It stirred a sense of camaraderie and respect within Reeves. These were not the daredevil thrill-seekers trying to exploit the mountain that Reeves anticipated. These were experienced, big mountain skiers, respectful of the mountain and its dangers. True, they were young, but they were also men who reached the rare point in maturity where youth merged with experience. Revolutions ignite from the sparks sprayed when bravado collides with wisdom. These are my people, Reeves thought, and he started to feel guilty over his duty.

"That's far enough, fellas," Reeves said, the strength of his voice projected over his reluctance. Reeves raised a hand, signaling the three young men to halt as he interceded. The young men stopped before him.

"This is a mountain. We're just here to ski, brother," the young man wearing a radio lanyard said, speaking for the group.

Reeves was taken aback. The young man said, "brother," not in wit, irony, or malice—he could not have known Reeves or his nickname—instead, the young man said it in a simple, fraternal tone. Reeves expected a confrontation with grievance and insults that accused him of being old, out-of-touch, and a sellout. He did not expect a plea that invoked a sense of camaraderie. And perhaps it was not a plea at all, but still, the words landed on Reeves' conscience and stirred his emotions. The words appealed to his emotions but not as an emotional appeal. They implored to that root which causes emotion—deep within Reeves, it was the mountain and what a man and his tools can do upon it. The emotion was not sympathy for the young men or their desires; Reeves felt aspiration for himself and his own. Reeves wanted to let them pass … to wish them well and give them blessings of safety … to let them attempt The Falls. He wanted to see them succeed.

"I can't let you do that," Reeves said, honoring his duty as a ski instructor under the employ of the mountain resort.

"There's no 'let' here, bluecoat," the young man chided. "We're hiking through those trees and skiing whatever it is that we find behind it. You can't stop all three of us."

"You're right. I can't stop you. And you know what, that mountain range back there, it can't stop you either. In fact, it won't stop you at all. It will let you pass, fall, and tumble while your body bounces off its iron rock."

"We've skied big mountains across four continents. We've made hundred-foot drops, skied a fifty-degree pitch, and succeeded where many men have died."

"Have you ever seen the terrain on the backside? I know you haven't because helicopters can't get in close enough to take photos, and hikers are not permitted in the wildlife sanctuary at the bottom. And for every man who's dared what you're trying, the mountain has taken his life in return. It's impossible."

"We have heard these arguments before, and they only motivate us. Everything's impossible until it isn't."

"The Falls are not a conquest, Reeves said. "It's a futile crusade. And to run it would be a miracle."

"Isn't that all the reason to dive in? To do the miraculous?"

"I want you to live."

"Living is trying to do something that's never been done. Death is living like an everyman. You say you want us to live. I say we want to be alive."

"You say that now. See how alive you feel when

you watch a friend perish on your ventures."

"Look at us, bluecoat. We've sat on flights with an empty seat next to us, having made arrangements for a brother's body to be shipped home. We know that hurt. And we know the aftermath. That pain is nothing next to the emptiness of going through life, knowing the feeling of making the first descent down a mountain that has never been skied before and ignoring the burning desire to find it again. We've all seen what's at the end of that path. You try to numb it because it never goes away. You try to fill it with alcohol and drugs and all those things that kill a man's spirit. That's not life. So we choose this, even if it means dying. Living otherwise is worse."

"I'm sorry, Reeves whispered and failed to find any other words to persuade the group.

The young man with the lanyard took the opportunity left by the pause. He gave a gentle jab with his elbow to each of his partners and signaled them with a nod to continue. They spread out, each treading toward a different entry in a tree line. Reeves stepped forward, raised his hands to his chest, and spread his elbows wide to block the young man with the lanyard. Their eyes locked, and neither man budged.

The young man shuffled to the side with

aggression to evade Reeves. The others rushed toward the forest. Reeves countered, colliding with the young man, who dropped his shoulder under Reeves's elbow. Reeves shoved him downward. The young man toppled onto one knee under the weight of his pack. Reeves lifted his hand off the young man's back, shaking his head in a self-reprimand for using force. He looked up and saw the others scrambling toward the trees. In a desperate plea—with a bleeding intention that wavered between stopping and helping the young men—Reeves shouted an involuntary bark, "You're going the wrong way!"

The group stopped, and the young man genuflecting under Reeves' arms looked up at him, first with curiosity and then with certainty as he said, "You've been back there before, haven't you?"

"Yes," Reeves said with reluctant guilt.

"But you didn't ski it."

"No, I didn't."

"Then help us succeed where you failed. Tell us where the access is."

"I can't," Reeves said, grabbing the young man's arm to help him up. The young man stood and met Reeves face-to-face.

"If you dared go back there, then you understand

why—why we're going," the young man said.

"I do," Reeves confessed, "but that doesn't change anything."

"It won't change anything for you. You went there, saw it, and balked. I can't help you get over your fear. We don't share your fear, bluecoat, and you have no right to press it upon us."

Reeves remained silent, struggling to say the words that he wanted to shout. His conscience fought the urge to tell the young men where to enter Hallow's Gallows; that the forest was just as steep as ski runs and, at times, they would need to climb backward and brace against tree trunks to keep from sliding down; that the only remote chance to survive was a vertical ridge protruding along the southmost portion of The Falls. He suppressed the words under the guise of his duty as a ski instructor, knowing, in truth, that his response was to the pressure of his own fear. He thought, I refuse to be responsible for these young men's deaths. Then, as if being answered by a ghost, the words, "We want to be alive," echoed in Reeves' mind. And he knew he would carry an even greater guilt should he strip these man of the responsibility of their own lives and their agency to pursue a passion.

"Okay," Reeves whispered to the young man, "I'll

tell you," but the admission was muffled by the spitting sound of a snowmobile engine. The roar caused the group to wince, and when their senses returned, the path to the Hallow's Gallows was blocked by the two patrollers who skied in from Head Lamp. Two others on snowmobiles surrounded the young men.

"That's enough," Jerison Foster said. He wore a red ski patrol jacket. Reeves recognized the voice from this radio.

"This is what is going to happen now," Pascal Moreau, Jerison's partner, said. "You're all going to turn around. We're going to escort you back to Head Lamp Gondola, where you will ride back down to the base. Your ski passes have been revoked. You are no longer permitted on this mountain. If there's any funny business, I'll have police waiting at the base. Try anything, and you'll be dragged off in handcuffs, wishing we had let you perish on the mountain today."

The young men's posture relented. The man with the lanyard looked in Reeves' eyes and shook his head in disappointment toward Reeves, himself, and all existence. Reeves froze and locked eyes with the skier, fighting his emotions and the urge to apologize. It was not empathy nor pity towards the skiers; Reeves held himself in silent account for his own actions. The young men turned around and hiked slowly as directed by the patrollers, with the two snowmobiles flanking either side of the group.

"Thanks for stalling them, Zack," Jerison said after the group dispersed. "It looks like things got a little tense here. You did good."

"Thanks for the reinforcements. You don't have to worry about the kids. They won't give you any problems."

"No? It looked like they were about to give it to you."

"They aren't troublemakers. They're purists, and they know they've missed their shot."

"All for the best. It was Enzo, by the way."

"Who, the kid?"

"No. Enzo Carabelli, the cat driver who dropped them off before the lifts opened. He's got the tab at The Steep Easy tonight. Drinks are on him."

Reeves nodded and walked back to his skis. They lay side-by-side with the poles planted in the snow next to the edge of either ski. The empty kit looked like a still photo of a phantom skier. Reeves moved with a somber walk to his equipment, moving like a man in torment.

"You saved their lives," Jerison said as he left to

catch up to the group.

Reeves mounted his skis, looked up to the soft gray of the snowy skies above, to the tips of the trees, and then his sight got lost in the dense hedgerow of Hallow's Gallows. A few hundred yards away from the drop of the cliff—which he imagined was covered by the same soft, dry snow for which The Seraphs were famous—drafted by nature and forever waiting for an expression made by the touch of a man.

"Is that what I did?" Reeves asked himself in rhetoric as his ski tips pointed to the flat safety of the marked trails.

Part Two: *The Sanctuary*

Stained glass windows split the late afternoon sunlight into the colors of a flame. The ambiance spread red and yellow hues over the decor of antique ski gear and mountain equipment, warming the guests of The Steep Easy in both body and spirit. Drinks and food were served to customers sitting at tabletops made of old wooden skis tiled together under a lacquer finish. Customers sat on old, repurposed chairlifts that bookended the bar's booths. After flying over the mountain, the Steep Easy provided a soft landing for skiers to welcome the evening.

The saloon doors swung and collapsed as Reeves entered the bar, passing a sign that read "Open Mic Night."

A man spoke into a microphone in the center of the bar's stage. He stood tall and proper with the collar of his black button-down shirt open and sleeves rolled up to his elbows. Every few moments, he glanced at the wire mesh of the windscreen as if to check that the microphone still worked. A spotlight steadied over a center stool, but the man paced about the stage, surrounded by three ranch-style fences with the bar's back wall completing the square. The smooth contours of the man's face and supple skin gave away his youth while his voice carried the weight of ages. No one in the crowd knew if the speaker was doing a stand-up bit or giving a lecture, nor did anyone pay attention long enough to determine which.

The ambient noise in the bar diluted the night's first performer while Zack Reeves took his perch on a barstool made of welded ski poles in a seat carved and polished from the wood of a used whisky barrel.

"What'll it be, *Brother Reeves*? The usual?" Michelle Strumgård asked Reeves from behind the bar. She wore a lined flannel shirt with cuffs folded back to avoid the backsplash from pouring drinks. Blonde locks of hair twisted with a ruby tint out of the bottom of her woolen hat, and her cheeks held the scarlet glow of a face fighting the cold—warm cheeks inside the frame of strawberry blonde hair. Her sight made Reeves feel at ease about the world and a distant uneasiness toward himself.

"Yes. Thank you, Chelle. And put it on Enzo's tab."

"You're the fourth person to order on Enzo's bill. He must have caused some real trouble out there today."

"Not exactly. He just…" Reeves' answer trailed off as he searched and failed to find the words for the day's events.

Michelle dried a glass and shelved it while Reeves sat in thought. She watched while Reeves stared at the mirror behind the bar. His periphery dissolved into a black shadow, which left a spotlight on his reflection. As his thoughts consumed more of his conscious, his vision barreled through his sight until all his eyes could perceive was a black void occupied by the singular memory of what he denied the three young men.

"Okay. Well, you sit here and think about it. It'll take a few minutes to get your order. I'll come back then, and we'll try this all over again," Michelle said and walked away to tend to the rest of the bar.

"Sorry, Chelle," Reeves replied after a moment before he snapped back into the present.

Reeves sat alone on his stool, struggling to keep his head up against the gravity to brood in his thoughts. He avoided the view of the mirror and searched the bar for a distraction. He fixed his attention on the stage when he noticed the young man speaking and pacing about the stage. Upon sight, Reeves wondered if the performer was of appropriate age to be in the bar. Upon listening, he heard a voice that was utterly inappropriate for the setting.

"…Some men preach caution against any leap to embrace Artificial Intelligence," Reeves heard the young man say in a voice that was clear, heavy, and devoid of disfluencies. "But the truth is, we've already made the leap. We repeatedly take this leap. We've leaped so many times in our history: when we first pressed a beam against a fulcrum; when we first felt the warmth from our own flame; when we first mounted a mule to carry our work; when we first split an atom and released its energy for human use; and so many others. AI was always a predictable chapter in the story of mankind. What we fear now is not the leap to AI but the height at which we soar from previous leaps. Our forebearers stood on the shoulders of giants. We cower at our own shadow. We are so far removed from our primal state where in every corner of the natural world hid an existential threat. We are a fragile species, destined for extinction if man had not discovered how to skirt evolution. We are the one species whose ingenuity exceeds impatience on the evolutionary scale. Thanks to human nature, we continually compensate for deficiencies in our environment and within our own biology.

"There's the rub: Human Nature. What is man's nature if not a constant pursuit to expand his capacity? Every tool ever built was designed with an intent to best man's strength, speed, precision, and production. Each breakthrough came with it a revolution of human flourishing thanks to the power of human thought. Why, our machines already reign superior to our memory and mathematical computation. Now, AI promises to eclipse the raw capacity of human thought. No, not even thought, our greatest evolutionary advantage, is exempt from our nature. The target was set the moment the first men began to reason. It's simply our next step. Now, we are at the precipice of a promise like no other in our history. A tool that can invent tools and draw abstractions too large and too minute for us to reach under the limits of flesh and time. My friends, imagine: the longest-standing questions, answered; the hardest problems, solved; and worst diseases, cured."

The young man paused at these words. His hand raised, and his eyes dropped until the two intersected before his face. His steadfast composure hid the flashing cycle of emotions. In one breath, he felt anxiety transform into fear, to relief, and finally to hope. He examined the microphone, relieved to find it held steady in his tight grip. In the next breath, a hand waved from the sound engineer's station, signaling the closing moment of the young man's stage time. He nodded and collected his final thoughts.

"Still, the warnings are many. Science fiction exhausted the examination of Artificial Intelligence as an existential threat—AI hijacks the military, a robot uprising enslaves humanity and the like. Like any art form, these works present to the faculties that inform human consciousness. We assume that a digital intelligence would hijack this physical world that hosts our bodies, our consciousness, from where we draw experience and our senses perceive. What's funny is we're drawing so many conclusions about a digital consciousness while we have so little knowledge of our own—but that is a different discussion altogether.

"These stories fail to ask the right questions. What is consciousness, and what form would it take in a neural processor? How would we recognize it? Would natural rights apply to it? And if so, at what point would it be considered a conscious and sovereign being? If a programmer starts writing a new algorithm and abandons it, is that tantamount to abortion? When an Artificial General Intelligence comes into being, what is its relationship to reality as an entity that experiences existence exclusively through electric currents and transistor gates? How would it consume knowledge and draw conclusions? Would it have any interest in humanity or our world at all when its experience is purely digital? Could it make judgments? Hold values? Experience emotions? Would it appreciate beauty? If it could only deal in cutthroat logic, would that perspective not compensate for humanity's tendency toward emotionally-drawn decisions? And if our creation does become the superior being, why would it not seek a mutually prosperous existence with us? Why would it not seek to teach and enlighten humanity? Why would it be any different than the billions of intellectually inferior life that we already share this planet with?

"Knowledge breeds courage, so these are the questions I ask, ponder, and seek to answer."

Reeves watched the young man's hand fall to his side and bow of his head. Nary a single clap recognized the end of the young man's set. The atmosphere continued of its own inertia, uninterrupted. Reeves expected to find disappointment in the young man's face but could not tell which was greater: the crowd's apathy toward the speaker or the speaker's indifference to the crowd. The young man raised his head until it tilted back over his shoulder blades. It conjured the image of an athlete's salute upon deliverance of a virtuoso performance. As he stood, it was clear to Reeves that the young man required no proof or recognition, as if his speech was meant to be unsung and preserved for his memory alone. With a single pose, the young man submitted to self-judgment and cast his verdict. The seed of pity planted in Reeves' stomach was quashed by the young man's posture, which had all the pride of a self-triumph made in solitude.

Reeves turned back toward the bar but found his attention stuck in the fog between memory and daydream. In his confusion, a thought transformed into a vision. Reeves saw himself holding the young man's pose as his own, standing in a deep valley and staring up a steep, bony mountain of sharp rock across its face. Only a single ridge of white snow ran down the vertical. The rock and snow cover was untouched, save for a single woven line crossing the spine of the ridge. The line quivered with symmetry across the vertex like the scaled pattern of a serpent's tail engraved on the mountain. The terrain was foreign; Reeves had never seen it before. The only familiarity was the suggestion of an exalted satisfaction that could only be held in silence. The feeling was distant but intimate, as if long-earned but never possessed. It took a moment for Reeves to realize that he was not reminiscing but imagining the memory of a long-held desire.

Before Reeves could reflect on the conjured image, he found the young speaker standing one seat over, leaning in with a raised finger, and signaling to Michelle that he wanted to order.

"You took the stage too early," Reeves told the young man when he noticed him. "In a couple hours and after a few rounds, they'll laugh and clap at just about anything coming off that stage."

"It doesn't matter if anyone listened or even heard me." The young man said.

"No? Why not?"

"It only matters that I stood and spoke. And that I delivered my words how I wanted."

"Seems odd. Why say them out loud and in a crowded bar, no less?"

"It's not so strange. We're in the middle of a mountain, right? What I did is not any different from skiing. You have to get out in the world to do it. And some days, you ski alone even if you're sharing the slopes with a crowd," the young man said.

"Fascinating," Reeves said, reacting to the discovery of his own thoughts inside the young man's words. "You don't sound like someone your age."

"I don't? Hmm. Perhaps some things age a man faster than time."

"Well said, old man, but if that's true, ought there also be things that restore a man's youth?"

"Well, this is interesting," Michelle's voice interrupted. "I have one man struggling to speak tonight, sitting next to another struggling to be heard." Michelle gestured to the young man, now sitting at Reeve's left at the bar. "What'll it be?" Michelle said.

"Double bourbon. On the rocks," the young man answered.

"Put it on Enzo's tab, Chelle," Reeves interjected.

"Are you sure, *Brother Reeves?*" Michelle asked with a slanted smile.

"Enzo should cover at least one real drink on my account."

"Coming right up," Michelle said and walked away to draw the liquor.

"Thank you, I guess. Or should I go find Enzo to thank him?" The young man said to Reeves as he swiveled his head about the room in an aimless gesture.

"I wouldn't advise that. Enzo isn't going to want to see anyone he's paying for tonight. Not unless you caught a ride up the mountain on a snowcat early this morning. Then he'd be keen to find you," Reeves said.

"No, I haven't skied yet. I just got in this afternoon, but now I'm curious why this Enzo would want to find me if I did."

"Enzo is a cat driver who drove some kids up the mountain before the lifts opened today. He probably thought they wanted to beat the crowds. Turns out the group snuck up early to attempt to ski *The Falls*. Me and a few patrollers had to intervene to stop them."

"What's a fall?" the young man asked—before Reeves could take a breath—in an immediate reaction that ignored the customary punctuation in casual conversation. He locked in on the words that Reeves did not mean to say.

"*The Falls*," Reeves emphasized. "I shouldn't tell you because they're a myth, a myth that's killed every skier who's chased it."

Reeves cast the words in an automatic reflex and without thought. The stern warning followed anyone who brought up *The Falls* in his presence. It took a moment for Reeves' thoughts to catch up to the moment, and he realized that he was the one who planted the question within the young man. The young man's gaze tightened on Reeves. Pupils dilate in the absence of light, amid darkness, perchance sight. And so it is for a man's mind. A question is an eclipse in the conscious, transforming the mind into an open expanse of possibilities. Reeves saw the spark of curiosity burning in the young man's face, which could only be extinguished by the satisfaction found in answers. Even more, Reeves knew that if a myth's allure lies in a mystery at its core that asks, "Is it true?" Knowledge, then, by implication, would erode its allure. If curiosity kills, then knowledge saves.

"Since you asked," Reeves continued. "And, judging by your speech tonight, I can see you'll keep asking until someone explains. So I'll tell you only as a warning. *The Falls* are a supposed ski run on the backside of the middle Seraphs," Reeves said, facing the young man. Reeves raised his arm, pointing past the door, the street, and the resort hotel toward the top of the mountain. His arm swooped down in a concave arc, falling below the bar top as he continued speaking, "The backside valley runs almost two thousand feet deeper than resort village.

Most skiers renown the front side of The Second Seraph as the best on-piste trails on Earth—that's why the pros train there. The backsides of the First and Fourth Seraphs are some of the best, most accessible off-piste skiing in North America. *The Falls* are an imaginary combination of both. Evangelists would convince you that it's a Shangri-La of virgin snow stretching eternally down a deep pitch. But in reality, it's a self-imposed sentence to agony. There's a thick forest between the mapped trails and the access. Beyond that, no one is sure. The land on the back side is a restricted federal wildlife sanctuary. You can't see down from the top or get close enough at the bottom to map a line down the run. Judging by the number of people who have died—there is none. It happens every year. I can't figure why people keep trying."

"Everything's impossible until it isn't."

"There's that youthful commentary from your generation again. What are you? Some kind of post-doc on your winter break? How old are you anyway?"

"I'm twenty-two. And I dropped out. I was a double major in computer science and philosophy, though."

"That explains your lecture tonight. People with

that kind of passion and ambition rarely give up. Why'd you quit?"

"You already noticed my contest with time. Let's say that I learn faster on my own."

"And you're in some kind of race to learn?"

"We all are."

"Is that right? What, then, are we all racing against?"

"A limited life span," the young man said in a tone so simple and clear as to suggest the answer was obvious.

"Hmm," Reeves said, thinking for a moment. "Maybe you do have something in common with that group I kicked off the mountain this morning."

"Very likely. But probably not in the way that you think."

"You two get even more interesting by the minute," Michelle's voice wedged into the conversation. "This is like the beginning of a joke. A nostalgist and a zealot are sitting at a bar."

Michelle raised an open palm toward Reeves and then to the young man. She stood for a moment as if expecting a response.

"What's the punchline?" the young man asked.

"I'm waiting to find that out for myself. What's your name, kid?" Michelle said.

"Aris Godric," he said, offering his hand to Michelle over the bar top.

"Of course it is," Reeves said under his breath.

"What's this?" Michelle asked, noticing a dark green script printed on the young man's forearm. She turned his hand to examine it. The script was illegible but elegant and drawn with impeccable symmetry.

"It's a verse written in a fictional language from an epic myth I read when I was twelve. This passage resonated with me immediately and grew more profound over the years. These words never fail to bring clarity when I face chaos in my life. I went back to read it so often that I had it inked on my arm so the words would always be with me."

"What does it say?"

"Oh no. It's just for me," Godric said, shaking his head with the bright smile of a man keeping a secret.

"You never share it?"

"I haven't yet. Maybe I'd share it with the right person at the right time."

"You know, it's quite annoying to put a secret on public display."

"That's funny," Godric's eyes shimmered with the glint of amusement.

"Why?"

"The hero in myth was the last of his kind. He was known as the Herald of Valor and lived by a code that held the nobility and honor of his people above everything, even his own life. The Great War purged his bloodline and rendered his code moot. Still, he recited the mantras and rituals. It often baffled and conflicted with people along his journey. Perhaps you, like those characters, are confusing annoyance with intrigue."

"Your hero sounds like someone I know, Michelle said, leaning over the bar and speaking with a coy whisper.

"I doubt it. Heroes like that don't exist in this world. Their place is in fantasy books," Godric said in fact.

"We'll see."

"I doubt it."

"What happens to the hero in your story?"

"The predictable. Myth becomes trope. The hero settled in a village and took up arms to protect it when invaders came to pillage their land. A farmer and his wife died in the battle. The hero adopted their orphaned son and raised him up according to his code. In the end, the hero fought alone against an army so that the boy might live."

"Is where you are from a secret, too?"

"Hardly. Wisconsin."

"Well, Aris Godric from Wisconsin. I'm Chelle, and this is *the Brother,* Zack Reeves."

"*Brother*? Are you some kind of monk?" Godric asked.

"He is," Michelle said, her voice involuntarily rising as she interjected on Reeves' behalf.

"Do you have our drinks yet?" Reeves said.

"Oh, yes. I have presents from Enzo. One for the past," Michelle said as she put a steaming styrofoam cup in front of Reeves. "And one for the future." Michelle set a glass of golden liquid poured over two frozen shards before Godric.

"Hot chocolate! You know this is a bar," Godric said, laughing.

"He's a skier to a fault," Michelle explained.

"You spend all day on the cold slopes, and you get to drink hot cocoa when you're finished." Reeves said as if reciting a creed.

"To a fault," Michelle emphasized as she stepped away to serve a new pair of customers who approached the bar.

"So what, do you live at a missionary nearby or preach at a local chapel?"

"I'm not a preacher like Chelle would have you

believe. I've been a ski instructor here for thirty years."

"So when they call you *brother*, it's because of how you teach," Godric concluded.

Reeves took a deep breath and forced an exhale that ended in a sigh. He wanted to ignore the comment, but there was something about hearing the words in Godric's speech that made Reeves wish to share his own. Thought provokes thought, and courage begets courage; when one man opens the depths of his mind to a public, it is an open dare for other men of deep musing. Even though Reeves did not understand Godric's heavy words, their mass connected to the weight of his own. So Reeves answered.

"At the beginning, it was because of the large classes that I taught," Reeves said. "So many enrolled in my sessions that the rest of the mountain staff said that I preached to a congregation."

"But something changed?" Godric asked.

"Skiing changed. Skiers aren't as concerned about technique because they don't have to be. Twenty years ago, a skier needed to build years of skill to control his equipment. Now, the equipment controls the skier. Just look at how specialized the equipment is. Find a man who picked the wrong skis for the conditions, and you'll find him flailing about the mountain and miserable. I'm a small minority who still wants to command the mountain through my skis—to know that no matter the lay of the snow, the angle of the pitch, or the temperature, I can ski it on my terms. That I can dictate to the mountain, to gravity, and to all the dangers that would be mortal without such control. I love to see and feel the beauty of perfect congruity between a skier's body and the slope. And I love to teach it. The culture of the sport is disintegrating that. It's all jumps, grinds, spins, and speed, if not bouncing off obstacles and other unnatural elements. They call it freestyle, which is appropriate because it's free of style."

"You sound like a bitter old man," Godric challenged.

"I know. I'm not though. The truth is I am grateful for every new trend. Each evolution brought more people to the sport. They saved the whole skiing economy more than once. Every generation seeks something novel, and with it, a new movement is born. I have seen it over and over again—from big mountain, to snowboarding, to terrain parks, to freeride. And I would never begrudge anyone who comes to the mountains in search of their own joy, whatever form that takes. But it's not what I fell in love with. For me, it's the beauty of control—the human body working in congress with the mountain through a pair of skis, the dictates of the mountain submitting to human will, finding the natural rhythm of the terrain, and making your own expression inside that space with precise and fluid movements—it's skiing as a hymn."

"Chelle was right. You are indeed a preacher. I'd hate to be a student in your class," Godric said, sipping his drink.

"You couldn't afford it. I stopped teaching groups about twelve years ago. Now, I only teach private lessons. All my clients are older and learned to ski as I did. Plus, they're wealthy—executives, industry moguls, trust fund heirs, and the occasional celebrity—and I charge them as such. I teach less and make more money than I ever have these days. And the lessons are more satisfying. With one student, I can witness improvement within one day, and most of my clients come back year after year so that satisfaction compounds."

"Teach anyone famous today?"

"No. I haven't taught a lesson in over a week. As good as this storm has been for the skiing, it's made the mountain passes almost undriveable for anything but large trucks."

"Don't I know it. I almost fish-tailed off the road a dozen times on my drive in."

"You're lucky you didn't crash."

"There were a couple of close calls. Thankfully, I happened upon a snow plow and slipped in behind it. It gave me a clear road to the village."

"That's some luck. Most would not have tried."

"People are trying. I'm sure they saw the snow reports like I did and dared the drive. I saw lots of abandoned cars stuck in the ditches along the roads."

"I'm not surprised. I check the ski school reservations every night. With conditions like they are, it's not uncommon for last-minute reservations. Some CEO will see the snow report and jump in his private jet to indulge the temptation."

"Are the conditions that good?"

"I've worked here for thirty years and have been visiting much longer than that. I can honestly say there has never been a winter like this year's nor a week like the one we're having. They say there's no such thing as perfection, and if not, then this is as close as The Seraphs may ever get."

"There's that word again," Michelle snuck into the conversation.

"You're such an instigator, Chelle. I need to stop

sitting at the bar," Reeves said.

"You wouldn't dare. You'd miss me too much," Michelle said.

"What word?" Godric asked.

Michelle lifted the black apron hanging below her flannel shirt and removed her mobile phone. She swiped her finger across the screen, smiling at an untold joke. Reeves blew across the top of his drink and watched the swirling steam dance in the air before returning to a thin strand, standing upon the liquid. He felt comfort in the warm air rising over his face and watched Michelle search her phone, knowing what she was doing without objection.

"'*So long as my breath shares same air that lays snow, I will seek perfection in every day, in every descent, and in every turn.*' You forgot to add, 'and I will end each day drinking hot cocoa at The Steep Easy,'" Michelle said, throwing Reeves' words at him.

"You said that?" Godric asked.

"He wrote that," Michelle said, handing her phone to Godric.

"'A More Perfect Pursuit,'" Godric saw the article that Michelle handed him and read the headline aloud.

Godric's face washed aglow in the shine of the

bright screen. His face was a proclamation of youth. Shadows clung to Godric's jawline, accentuating his pinched brow and stretching the gaunt lines of his cheeks, and his eyes studied the article with the energy and focus reserved for the young. Spry in both body and mind, Godric exhibited the speed at which a young man's interest can shift from piqued to obsessed. Godric's glance narrowed as he read aloud:

"'I've found no greater reward than the moment my foot slides into the pillowy softness of my sneakers after spending the daylight inside the hard, stiff polymer of a modern ski boot. The immediate relief is the shadow from a flash of memories that instantly and simultaneously recall the pressure I felt atop every turn, the turbulence of my skis clapping against an unexpected ice patch, the weight of my skis dangling beneath a chairlift, and the strength of my long battle to tame both the mountain and gravity. Their indivisible sum is a rapture and equaled only by that tranquility I'm granted when I trade my boots for shoes. I may not have succeeded in my battle, but I tried. And every day I try is better than the day before it. So chances are, if you see me out on slopes, you found me on the best day of my life.'"

"Amen, *Brother*," Michelle said. Her volume dropped with each syllable, and her playful banter waned, unable to hide her sincerity, her admiration for the words and the man who wrote them.

"When did you write this?" Godric asked as he read the article a second time.

"Maybe twenty years ago. An editor from Squall Magazine reviewed our ski school and joined one of my classes. Afterward, he asked me to write an editorial about why I teach. I always understood it but never described my why in words before. Once I started writing, I couldn't stop. That's what came out. I'm not sure I answered the original question, but Squall published it."

"You answered it better than they could have hoped," Godric said.

The murmur of the bar filled the quiet interlude that followed. Each of the three consumed the moment in their own way. Godric continued reading the article, pausing occasionally as if to cauterize a note in his mind. He finished and laid the phone on the bar top near Michelle. Reeves's head fell backward while a stream of hot cocoa warmed the back of his throat. Michelle watched them both and remembered why she liked being a bartender in the ski village.

Michelle glanced across the counter to find full glasses in front of her customers engaged with their friends. Laughter lifted over smiling faces with occasional chimes of kissing glasses in cheers, commemorating a day of epic skiing. With no new orders, she leaned against the bartender's ledge across from Reeves.

"You know, he asks me to ski with him from time to time," Michelle said to Godric. "I saw him making laps on The Fourth Seraph by himself today. Maybe you can find out why he doesn't invite me to join him when he's not teaching."

"Is that so?" Godric said, playing off Michelle's setup. "What is it, *Brother Reeves*? Does Chelle not meet your lofty standards? Is she not good enough to ski with you?"

Michelle's mouth fell to an open smile. She was as surprised as she was pleased by the stranger's audacity.

"Oh, I like this one! Yes, please answer the question," she said, turning to Reeves, waiting for his response.

"Using the kid to do your dirty work, Chelle? That's a lawyer's trick," Reeves said, "I should have seen that coming."

"You're evading the question."

"Just like you're evading that gentleman waiting to order a drink," Reeves said, pointing to a new customer at the far end of the bar.

"Saved by commerce. To be continued," Michelle slapped her hands against the bar top and scurried away to help the customer.

"She's something else," Godric said to Reeves and indulged a small dose of his drink.

"Yes, she is," Reeves said, again staring at his reflection in the mirror.

"You have some real chemistry with her."

Reluctance is a stoic folly, a symptom of a frozen mind amid the swirl of dissonant thoughts. Reeves did not respond, and the contemplation on his face let Godric know that he should not press. Reeves' desire for Michelle sunk in his subconscious, chained to the anchor of conflicting thoughts: the words he wrote and a perfection that he strived for but could not reach; and what he took from the group of skiers that morning in front of the backdrop of Hallow's Gallows. He was not aware of the link between those truths and his feelings for Michelle, but those feelings breached at unpredictable moments when he'd reach out to her to spend a winter day on the slopes or a summer day hiking the foothills. And why he ended every night sipping his warm drink in her presence.

"She is a wonderful skier," Reeves avowed, addressing the accusation that his conscience could not leave unresolved. "As playful as she is in her bar, she's even more so on the slopes. Skiing with her is…" Reeves said, but his words dissolved into a thought he could not admit.

"A joy," Godric said, completing the sentence.

"Yes."

"Does she know that?"

"She knows well the kind of skier she is."

"Does she know you think it?"

"Yes," Reeves said in a manner that was more hopeful than certain.

The pair sat in silence in the following moments. Godric lifted his glass and extended it to Reeves, saying, "Here's that which brings us joy."

"Cheers," Reeves said. Clear glass met white foam as the two lifted their heads to the sky and drained what was left of their drinks. Godric felt the bourbon burn down his throat, while Reeves savored the sweet taste of chocolate and the new warmth in his stomach. The glimpse of tossed heads is a universal invitation for a bartender, and Michelle found her way back to the pair.

"Can I get you boys another round of comfort?"

Michelle asked, examining their empty cups.

"If I wanted comfort, I would have what he's having,' Godric said.

"Now you're talking like a skier. But nothing for me, Chelle. I am going to be on my way. Get the kid another drink on Enzo's tab. Then cut him off," Reeves said with a wink.

"Oh, you can't let him off the hook like that," Godric said.

"He knows he's never off the hook. Good night, *Brother*," Michelle said.

"'Till next time," Godric said, nodding a salute toward Reeves.

Reeves left a tip on the counter large enough to cover any objections from Enzo, grabbed his jacket, and was outside the Steep Easy before he clasped it over his chest. The last bit of daylight pooled in the valley as the sun slipped below the range line's western edge. A lifetime at The Seraphs could not acclimate Reeves to the disorienting flow of time in a ski town. An early start and hard runs exhaust a man by the time the lifts close. When the first round gets ordered at four o'clock, five PM feels like midnight. The remaining twilight and lighted streets surprised Reeves when he exited the Steep Easy, and the winter air brushed across his face and soaked into his open jacket. His cheeks tingled, and his nose throbbed as the chill dripped down his neck and sent a shiver through his sternum.

The cold air stirred Reeves' thoughts, agitating a spectrum of emotions. Cold is dynamic therapeutic. Frigid air can soothe and relieve; it acts as a numbing agent, or it can be its own piercing pain. It can preserve a life on the brink of death, and it can kill off its own accord. Cold can sedate a man or shock him into action with a rush of adrenaline. Reeves walked, tucking his hands deep into his pockets as the dusk evaporated in the final moment where shadow transformed into night. Reeves knew somewhere in the valley three men cursed him. Three men who were right to both curse and indebt him, whom Reeves himself condemned and whose lives he saved. He was not sure which to regret or to celebrate.

As Reeves approached the parking lot, a buzz in his pocket broke the spiral of thoughts. He looked down and saw the familiar number from the ski school office. He answered and greeted the booking agent.

"Hello, Holly," Reeves said into his phone.

"Are you able to take a client tomorrow?" the booking agent asked.

"Yes. No problem. Who is it for?" Reeves snapped automatically.

"It's a new client. I only have a callback number. I waited to collect booking details until I could confirm with you. He asked for you specifically."

"Okay. Book the appointment and let him know where and when to meet me. I'll log on in the morning to check the details."

Reeves tucked the phone back in his pocket, unlocked his door, and climbed into the cab of his utility vehicle. The steady snow blew across the road and through the shine of Reeves' headlights. Snowflakes flashed through the beams, appearing and disappearing in brilliant streaks like a shower of shooting stars. Reeves' mind began to quiet down, thinking of the familiar routine he would observe the night before a lesson. The car warmed to a comfortable temperature, and his breath slowed to a peaceful cadence. When his thought returned, he realized who had booked the lesson.

"That old son of a bitch," Reeves whispered to himself with a quiet laugh.

Part Three: *The Ministry*

The steady hum of the space heater erased the silence but could not fend off the cold inside Reeves' garage. 6:18 AM flashed on the old clock radio resting on the workbench. The time was the only evidence of the morning hours. The windows remained dark, and Reeves left a steaming mug of coffee next to the hot iron to keep warm. He sat on a round stool, reached for the mug, and felt the cold metal seat stealing warmth from his legs. A ski lay upside-down, trapped in a pair of vices affixed to the tabletop. A recessed light left a halation around the open cabinet secured against the wall. Reeves considered its contents.

He took a long, slow sip from the mug. He cradled the warm glass and relished the contrast of warmth radiating under his palms against the prickling chill biting his knuckles. The open forecast on his phone showed a temperature of twelve degrees Fahrenheit with a high of twenty. He pulled a red bar of wax out of the cabinet, set it away from the hot iron, and examined his skis one last time.

Meticulous care kept his equipment fresh. The base of the skis were unblemished, clean, and as virgin as the day he received them. He ran a soft nylon brush across the mounted ski, followed by delicate cloth. They both ran smooth, without snagging or bunching, as if he were brushing velvet. Reeves folded the cloth, placed it on the workbench, and then sat still, stretching one moment into the next. A craftsman does not do a task a thousand times to become a master. Mastery comes by performing a task once, a thousand times over. So it was with Reeves.

The iron and wax rose together with Reeves as he pressed the red bar against the hot metal. He held the pair over the workbench and watched the bar molten and drip onto his ski. The wax liquified against the iron, leaving no trace of smoke. The aroma of a dull, aged must plumed throughout the garage. Reeves continued. He christened the ski, crossing back and forth against the ski's backplane in a slow, methodical motion. The maroon drizzle solidified against the cool, white surface as if each drop codified a covenant. After covering the base top-to-bottom, he ran the iron across the mounted ski, spreading the wax in an even film, leaving the bottom covered in a pool of red and intentions to bond with the skis. He repeated the process with his second ski with the same meticulous care as if performing the task for the first time.

Reeves pulled a thin blade across the surface, shaving off the bulk. The thin strips of wax fell in curling ribbons over the tabletop until no trace of the red wax could be seen. Still, the oil filled and anointed the deep pores in the ski's surface. They felt smooth against Reeve's fingertips and would pass as silk over the day's cold snow. Reeves locked the long planks in the rack on the roof of his car to keep them as cold as possible. The routine kept his skis ripe and prepared his mind. Reeves packed the rest of his gear, ready for whatever he might find on the mountain.

Flurries twirled in the gentle breeze, invoking the image of a living spirit that hovered over Head Lamp Gondola. The motion was precise, almost deliberate, as thin waves of snowfall defied gravity, fluttering in a mesmerizing adagio. A small queue of skiers marched through roped-off lanes, waiting for the operator to open the gondola and the mountain to the riders. Reeves brushed off a pillow of snow nestling on his shoulder as he stood near the empty ski school lane. His skis leaned against the other shoulder, stretching over Reeves' head, its tips a few inches closer to the sky.

Reeves looked for Godric among the early skiers

who braved the frosty morning. The zipper of his signature parka pressed against his chin. The bound collar proved an effective shield against the cold air. Only Reeves' cheeks felt the pinch of winter. The jacket radiated its glacial-blue tone, not a reflection of an ice sheet but of the glowing sapphire core deep within a blue-iced glacier. Reeves' eyes panned across the flat, snowy plane between his station, the lodge, and the parking lot. The assembly of skiers preparing for the day grew even in the few moments Reeves observed. A steady flow of guests exited the resort and gathered their equipment at the ski corral. A stream of visitors passed through the ticket lines, already donning their helmets and goggles as a barrier to the freezing temperature. Local pass-holders sat at benches or on the snow, tightening their boots after trekking through the parking lot.

Among the growing mass, a skier wore a fluorescent jacket, gleaming like an electric current running through ripe orange rind.

The jacket left the impression of an accent mark on the skier. His shape and movement should have blended into the surroundings, but the color was a distinct tone that left the skier insoluble to the setting. He carried his skis over his shoulder and moved through scattered patches of light and shade.

The Sun had crept over the tips of The Seraphs, casting broken shadows over the plane, and as he moved, the skier's jacket flickered like the burning ember atop a charred, flaming candle wick. Reeves watched the man in an innate response. Man's instinct calls his eyes to fix upon a flame and hold its sight until he is hypnotized by its wafting spires. So it was that Reeves' attention latched upon the skier. He watched in contemplation while the skier approached with a direct resolution. A hint of familiarity kindled Reeves' mind as he reclaimed his senses from the short trance. When the skier spoke, his voice thrust Reeves from familiarity into full recognition. He expected to find Godric looking for him, and Reeves should have expected to find him just as awkward in sight upon the slopes as he was in sound during his lecture at The Steep Easy.

"I'm here for ski school," Godric smirked.

"Where's your rifle? You look like you're ready for a biathlon," Reeves said, raising his ski poles toward Godric's jacket with his ski poles.

"That's funny," Godric replied with a chuckle that absorbed Reeves' playful reproach.

"Last night you were lecturing in a bar, and now this," Reeves continued to gesture at Godric's outfit. "You do like to stand out, don't you?" Reeves said.

"I like to stand straight." Godric said with a pause, then added, "And mean it."

"You can stand straight in any jacket."

"Not exactly. Form follows function. You wear a sports coat in an office, military fatigues on the battlefield, and a speed suit on a race course. Can a man truly stand if he'd not selected appropriate dress?"

"What a thing to say and of all places to say it. Here, nothing is inappropriate. The absurd is the expected. I've seen skiers in spiked Mohawks, onesies that look like astronaut suits, and tourists skiing in jeans. You can pick any of a hundred ski coats that keep you warm and allow proper movement."

"Yes. And I chose this one."

"Why?"

"Because I like it."

The answer was so simple and clear that it shocked Reeves. Godric offered no other rationalization for his choice, and Reeves understood, needing no further explanation.

"Here, hand me those," Reeves said as he extended his hand to take Godric's skis.

The gondola carriages circled the loading area without riders as part of their daily check-up and maintenance. Tim Garrick manned the operator's station in front of a control board lined with green lights, indicating that the lift and all the carriages were ready for riders. Garrick basked in the final moment of stillness before opening the gates for the flood of skiers expected all day. A large speaker streamed a guitarist playing in double time, and Garrick bounced to the rhythm in his standard mountain staff uniform: a forest-green parka with black pants. When he saw an instructor carrying two pairs of skis up the ski school lane, he left his station to meet Reeves and Godric at the front of the line. Garrick gave Reeves a nod of approval to pull the lane maker open and approach the gondola. Garrick gave the benefit and honor of a head start to instructors accompanied by paying customers.

"We good to ride up, Tim?" Reeves said.

"By all means. Welcome to The Seraphs." Garrick answered Reeves and offered his salutations to Godric.

Godric climbed into the next cabin as it crawled through the loading area. Reeves followed, dropping the skis into the rack next to the doors as he entered. Godric propped his arms against his knees on the back bench to face the mountain's four peaks. Reeves sat with his back toward the mountain and watched the growing line of skiers fall below them as they rose. The ride was smooth, and the gondola's sharp ascent felt like a hoist shooting up the side of a skyscraper. Their gondola dipped at the midpoint between two pylons. The lines held taut and steady, yet a slight tremor shook the cabin and surprised Reeves. He wondered for a moment what the inspection team had missed before he noticed Godric's leg bouncing incessantly. He recognized the nervous symptoms.

"Is this your first time skiing The Seraphs?" Reeves asked, knowing the answer.

"It is. I've skied most of the areas on the eastern ridge but never managed to visit anything in the deep range. It gets expensive with the extra day of travel, car rental, gas, and lodging fees," Godric said.

"Not to mention, when you get here, the hotels and rentals don't measure up to the luxury of the major resorts. The average tourist won't find that comfort here. Skiers come here to ski. No one visits on accident. That's one of the reasons that I call this mountain the best in North America."

"I didn't realize the ride up is steeper than a rollercoaster."

"The mountain is an interesting mirage. From the

base, it is tall and majestic. The groomed paths almost look like characters etched into the mountain, as if some ancient civilization left a poem in hieroglyphs on the slopes. But when you get up close and start the ascent, it becomes an animal baring its teeth—except it's the sharp gradient climb that sends the fierce warning to approachers."

"Ever have someone bail out and just ride the gondola back down?"

"No. Not after reaching the far side of the mirage. Up near the top, that sense of danger transforms into temptation. Every skier of worth thinks he can tame it. The wild mountain provokes him to become just as feral. I've never had someone walk away from that. I don't know why anyone would."

"Only if they're forced, like that group you said tried to ski *The Falls*," Godric said and listened carefully to Reeves's response.

"Only if they're forced." Reeves repeated in a whisper and stared out the gondola window.

The base of the mountain disappeared behind the frozen fog of snowfall. The air was filled with an ivory plume, and the ground covered in chalk. The Gondola seemed suspended in a white void of pure promise that would have inspired even a muse. Reeves stared at the distance behind and saw, clearly in his mind, the three men being escorted away from Hallow's Gallows, living with the consequences of his choice.

Introspection negates suggestion. Reeves's aimless stare let Godric know that Reeves saw his thoughts with more clarity than his vision, and any attempts to solicit further information on *The Falls* would fail. Godric did not press further but placed a bookmark on a thought to be resumed later.

In the quiet, Godric noticed his trembling knee and pulled his hands against his legs. He questioned and then assured himself that he had taken a double dose of his medication with his breakfast, and his twitching legs were but a release of nervous energy. Godric gripped his limb as if touching it was a reminder that it was his and that self-contact gave him a deeper connection and control over his body. He kept the pose for a moment, his hands spread wide like a mystical healer granting health to a broken bone. When he released his leg, the heavy boot anchored to the floor, and his leg held steady as its taught chain.

The jitter left the cabin, leaving only a gentle wave to rock the gondola as it swung gently as a pendulum above the mountain. The mind of an expert assimilates action and memory, and the familiar cadence ignited Reeves' mind. The lesson began.

"I am going to demand a lot out of you today," he said. "I'm not sure you knew exactly what you signed up for when you booked me, but you have. So you will get the full experience. You're new, and I do not typically get new clients, especially ones who haven't sought me out to teach my style and way of skiing," Reeves said in the manner of a teacher setting classroom expectations on the first day of school.

"What way is that?" Godric asked.

"I will teach you to be an aesthete," Reeves said, adding the hint of a French accent on the last word. "All my contemporaries will teach you techniques that keep both skis independent to take advantage of modern equipment. It makes it easier to recover from mistakes and, thus, easier to ski. I make it harder. I will teach you to keep your skis, ankles, and knees as tight as possible, where your entire body moves in unison as a single entity. It's difficult and takes years to master. You may not enjoy it. This is not the best mountain to learn on. The other instructors say that my style is inefficient. They'd tell you to hire them instead. They're cheaper and will argue that you'll enjoy your vacation more. They're probably right, too."

"Then why teach this style at all?"

"Have you ever seen someone ski as I described?"

"Yes. It's rare, and they're usually older. But you can't miss them."

"Why?"

"I suppose it's because it looks like they're flaunting or grandstanding."

"Right. We're show-offs. That's the reaction we get. They say we're stubborn, and our style is smug. Most skiers are resentful, even if they don't realize it."

"That's true. Why is that?"

"On the surface, it's because our skiing is fluid, and that gives it beauty. It makes others ugly and awkward by comparison. But the deeper reason is that we do not care about our appearance or other skiers. They judge us, but we grant no merit to their judgment. We seek not their acceptance nor refute their rejection. If we looked down upon other skiers, we'd be more accepted. We do not, and that's why we appear conceited and condescending. Isn't it funny how hatred is preferable to indifference? We're indifferent to other skiers because it's the experience we are after. I mentioned how your body must act in unison with this style, but it's more than that. Your body, your motion, your skis, your path over the snow, the line you choose, the pull of gravity against your mass, your entire universe converges, and everything else disappears. And when you master it, your conscious holds command over it all. The entirety of existence becomes self-contained to you and your line and subject to your will, like Michelangelo beholding a block of raw marble or Tchaikovsky peering upon a silent piano."

"Now, you're saying skiing is an art form?"

"Certainly. As much as dancing is an art."

"But a dance is set to music. A dancer's movements correspond to the rhythm and melody. That doesn't exist in skiing."

"My friend, what do you think the mountain is?"

"An aesthete," Godric said, connecting his teacher's question to the broader lesson. Reeves bowed his head in approval and in reverence.

"Yes. Just like a dancer and a gymnast. A herald of beauty," Reeves added.

Reeve's reference to Godric's epic myth added new punctuation that left the lesson lingering in his student's mind. Godric stared out the window, thinking of the script on his forearm and contemplating his teacher's words. He watched the thinning snowfall dissolve into tiny speckles of glimmering dust that bejeweled the space between the carriage and the ground. The sunlight pierced the clouds with beams that glazed the slopes. Godric looked at the empty trails below, and, in the deepest corners of his conscious—in his soul—he heard them asking, pleading for a new expression: to be ridden, to be conquered, to be enjoyed.

"When we get out, veer hard left. We're going to take Speedway as our first run. It's steep, but the staff groomed it overnight. The fresh snow will give you a good stage," Reeves said, giving his next instructions of the lesson.

"A stage for what?" Godric asked.

"To show me what kind of skier you are."

Head Lamp Gondola's climb stretched nearly two-thirds of the mountain from the base, where Reeves and Godric unloaded. The pair stood with their skis at rest at the crest of Speedway's descent. Reeves led Godric through a series of motions and poses that mimicked the mechanics of his skiing style. Godric listened to his instructor. Reeves demonstrated the posture. The muscles in his legs pulled tight through each pose, and his joints relaxed and opened. His body stretched to the extent of his surroundings, which Godric could not help but admire.

"Ready?" Reeves asked.

Godric nodded and turned toward the slope. The border of dense trees and shape of the terrain obfuscated the rest of the mountain so that all Godric could see in his immediacy was the Speedway's open path. The base village and the entirety of the valley remained hidden. The only hint of a path down was the steep drop-off, where the path disappeared in the distance. Beyond the valley, sprawling mountains stacked upon mountains filled Godric's vision, and he felt safety under their protection—not from any dangers within nature, which were abundant, but from the perils of man. The wicked are lazy and short-sighted, and Godric thought that no evil would dare traverse that labyrinth. Reeves stood straight and extended his hand, first to Godric, then sweeping his palm toward the open slope. Accepting Reeves' invitation, Godric stepped into his bindings.

"You lead," Reeves instructed. "Take the run all the way down until you hit the crossway between a trio of chairlifts. Stop there, and we'll take one of them to another part of the mountain. I will watch you from behind. When you start, I want you to feel the mountain and find its rhythm in your turns. Make your turns like a drum beat: boom-boom-

boom-boom." Reeves continued, bouncing his shoulder and striking his hand forward with each imagined beat.

Godric inched forward until his feet reached the cornice, and a length of his ski hung over the edge. His back and arms shuttered as a rush of energy raced through the marrow of his bones. The long, open path was empty and offered him the freedom to choose any line he wished. The sharp drop itself held a charisma normally reserved for a temptress that called to Godric as if to say, dive in and see what desires I might satisfy.

With a shove of his poles, Godric dropped onto the slope. The mountain granted instant speed as if acceleration were superfluous, and crossing the threshold was enough for Godric to reach his peak velocity. The light powder parted around his skis and lifted Godric's mass as he floated over the fresh snow. It was only when he pressed his skis to turn that he found the hard, packed piste just below the soft cover. As Godric pushed his edges against the slope, the mountain met him as a willing partner, grabbing his edges and pushing him through his turns. Skimming across the snow, Godric pushed himself to ski harder and faster, and the more he pushed, the grander his intention, the more the mountain would respond in kind. He flexed his muscles, and the mountain made them stronger.

He swept back and forth, each turn cascading into the next in a congruous flow. The harmony lifted his aged thoughts, exposing his youth and its infinite energy—he thought it a gift, not to be missed, nor to be squandered—and feeling a love rooted in praise for himself and in gratuity to the mountain. He moved without thought or consideration, his motion following a constant theme and expressing a single truth: this is the best I have ever skied.

The run seemed endless, and his speed infinite. He thought for a moment that if he skied any faster, the wind would lift his body to carry him off into the sky. He was mesmerized by his own ability, such that he was unsure what came first: the sound, the sight, or the shattering of his confidence. All three exploded as Reeves cruised ahead of him.

Reeves skied on muscle memory and passed Godric without effort. His years spent tinkering and improving transformed the musculoskeletal into the metellomechanical. Reeves was a machine, a machine carefully adapted to ski, and more, to ski The Seraphs. His form was taut and unwavering, but Godric saw that Reeves skied in reservation of his full capacity. He watched his instructor pass him with a nonchalance that insinuated nothing but insults, not realizing that the ridicule was but a reflection of his own thoughts. Reeves called out commands as he strolled past his student with casual speed and in complete control. Hear the screaming. "Knees forward … Shoulders back … Pull your feet together … Press into the turn, pop up across the peak … Get your hands out in front of you … Anticipate your turns … Plant your poles!"

Godric absorbed the instructions and put them into practice. He pulled his skis together and pressed over them. He felt betrayed by the mountain and by his body. The harder he forced his skis into a straight line, the more they would tend to a parabola, bowing outward then curling back. He watched his skis carefully and saw them wobble as he tried to hold them steady. As he neared the bottom, his skis crossed over each other. Seeing the trouble, Reeves slowed his skis and pulled away from Godric's line. Godric's ski tips clashed. His balance shattered along with his confidence. Thrashing arms stretched upward and out; he grabbed at the sky as if the air held his lost balance. His skis slipped about the icy ground in a countermotion to every movement of his libs. Godric's torso teetered, finding no support between the baseless air and the slick ground. He braced to fall, extending his arms to catch himself and throwing his leg in the opposite direction. The sudden jolt untangled his skis, split them apart, and forced Godric to shift all his weight onto his downhill ski, lest he tumble altogether. His far edge shaved and then cut into the frozen ground, creating and following its own self-made track. The rigid strength of the ski cut into the mountain and pulled a thread of stability through Godric's leg and up through his chest. His body straightened, and his skis followed.

The slope flattened, and Godric coasted until he came to rest upon the center junction between the three chairlifts. Each lift spawned toward a different area of the mountain. Godric spun his head in confusion over the unknown paths and the fragility of his confidence. The sudden loss of control made him feel as foreign in his own body as he did in the territory. The familiar terror made him raise his hands and pretend to adjust his gloves, expecting to find the latent tremor active in his hands. His hands kept steady, his poles hanging gently around his wrists. He squeezed his hands into a fist. Power rushed from the contraction of his forearms through each fingertip that dug into his palm. Strength drives resolve—and it gave Godric relief. The dread of exile from his own body always loomed, but this time, he could not blame his symptoms. He lost control; it was not taken from him. The speed at which it happened left him shaken. As he skied, he felt not only that he performed his personal best but that he poked at man's peak capacity on skis. But a feeling is just that. In the span of a moment, he collapsed from virtuoso to novice … from novice to plebe … from skiing in concert with the mountain to falling as its victim. As Godric's head swiveled in appraisal of the three lifts around him, he thought Reeves would direct him to the ride that would drop him on the easiest run, and Godric silently wondered which would lead him off the mountain altogether.

Reeves curled around Godric in a soft landing. His feet played axle in a final pivot as he spun around Godric until the two men stood face-to-face. The short plane between them split reality like a prism. Reeves in his customary blue and Godric in his unorthodox orange looked like opposite sides of an inverted mirror. Their faces substantiated the division. Godric's eyes hid behind his visor, refusing to hold any vision and finding only disappointment and doubt wherever he gazed. Reeves raised his goggles, and his eyes locked onto his student above a smile that made no attempt to hide his delight. Godric saw his teacher's response and felt ashamed.

"Nice run. How'd that feel?" Reeves said with a spark of enthusiasm that ignited the shame fueling Godric's mind.

"How do you think it felt? My skis crossed over each other, and I was an inch away from tearing my knee and breaking my arm," Godric replied.

"You're too hard on yourself. You made a nice recovery."

"I'm too hard on myself? I don't think you found one aspect of my technique satisfactory. You criticized everything."

"That's because you are a great skier."

Godric fought the urge to curse his teacher, believing that the compliment sprouted from an infertile ground. He expected scrutiny and would have accepted any insults aimed at his skiing, conceding that his near-fall had painted a target and invited such insults. Even in the moments before—when the high speed and steep terrain obeyed him just as his arms and legs, and his skis and poles followed his command—Godric's ability brought only a challenge from his teacher, followed by a litany of criticism. Reeves set the stage and challenged Godric to demonstrate what kind of skier he is. He failed and could accept any judgment so long as it conferred penitence and delivered a verdict of guilt. The praise lashed Godric's pride with a snap of condescension. Godric's brow scowled beneath his helmet and mask with a growing animosity intended for his teacher; however, when Godric raised his eyes, he found no sign of deceit or posturing in Reeve's demeanor. Reeves' entire disposition was that of a man whose ravage curiosity found utter—and honest—satisfaction. The persistent smile held as Reeves leaned on his poles and looked at his student against the frame of the mountain as if his sight not only granted him his immediate vision but the powers of a prophet with a complete image of the day to come.

"I almost fell, coach," Godric snapped.

Godric spoke with restraint but without composure. He referred to Reeves as "coach," but Reeves distinctly heard the intention Godric projected into the title as if to say, "You bastard."

"If you're not close to falling, you're not getting better," Reeves said, responding to what was said and addressing what went unsaid.

"You never see great skiers on the verge of crashing."

"No? Follow me."

Reeves sped off to one of the lifts without looking back. Godric rushed to catch up to him and slid in next to Reeves just as the next chair swung around to pick them up. Godric was surprised to find Reeves securing the safety bar over them not even a moment after clearing the loading zone. The lift carried them across The Second Seraph as it climbed from the base to the northern peaks. The ride ferried them over Mine Bender, where skiers from the national team took warm-up runs ahead of their training. Reeves nudged Godric's shoulder and pointed his attention to the racers zooming below them.

"Those are some of the best ski racers in the world. Each one of them spent their life skiing and have at least a decade of racing experience. You know what they're trying to do when they practice?"

"They're trying to get faster."

"That's true, but think about how they are doing that. A race is all constants: the course, the equipment, the technique are all the same."

"It's execution, is what you're telling me?"

"That's part of it. But what is that execution? These guys reach a hundred miles per hour. They're up on the cutting edge of their skis. If something goes wrong, if they catch an edge, hit an unexpected ice patch, or if their equipment malfunctions, do you think they stand a chance to recover?"

"No."

"Exactly. You said you never see great skiers on the verge of crashing. I say that the very best skiers only ski that way. Keep an eye on that racer in the red suit and green bib at the starting line." Reeves said, pointing to a skier stretching near the starting line. "That's Knute Levy, the best skier on the team. He'll tell you that in ski racing, you win in the margins, and those margins are infinitely slim. To win, you have to be more daring than the next man, so racers push themselves as close as they can to crashing out. A good racer will ski within an inch of his life. The next will come within a millimeter. A champion, like Knute, will be a micron away from his grave if he is to climb to the top of a podium. When you see training like this, it's proof that becoming a better skier means stretching beyond your limit.

"You almost fell. So what? Do you realize that you got to that point not when I started giving you instructions but when you started following them? The moment you began to do the work to get better is when you started to fall. Do you understand that?"

Reeves said.

Godric thought while his eyes locked on the red and green skier racing below the starting gate. Godric watched the racer's controlled speed, carving hard into the mountain through a tight turn. Godric turned his shoulders and leaned over the back of the chairlift to watch the racer after the lift passed the race course. The racer cut around the corner, his edges cut into the mountains as the plane of his skis stood almost upright against the slope. The skier's legs stretched parallel, with only a thin plane separating the racing suit from the snow. Godric could almost feel his own core burn as the racer braced his torso to keep his shoulders from rubbing against the snow. The skier straightened his turn and launched into the air just before he dropped over a ridge and slipped out of sight.

"I understand. And I'm sorry." Godric said, apologizing for his reaction and the unspoken words.

"This is a good thing. Now that I know what kind of skier you are, we might actually have some fun today."

"What do you mean?"

"It snowed all night and all week, for that matter. Since I know you can handle it, we're hitting the backside of The Fourth Seraph and heading over to ski Offering Bowl for the day. There's nothing like it in the east-range hills that you've skied. It will be the best skiing of your life."

With a complete plan, Reeves looked ahead, anticipating his next lesson. Godric continued to watch the race course, where he saw the odd sight of a skier with three skis dashing between the gates. He examined the skier and realized that it was not a man with three skis but a racer with one ski and a set of outriggers—arm braces affixed with a mini-ski at the end. The amputee challenged the race course with all the aggression, skill, and speed of any other racer at practice. Godric heard Reeves preach about using his two skis as a single plane and thought: here's a man with no choice but to ski on a single plank or not ski at all. He's lucky, Godric concluded, that whatever tragedy took his leg still left him with a choice. The lift climbed beyond Mine Bender's view, and Godric thought about his own fate, wishing he could trade it for the para-skier's.

A sign reading "Independent's Day" with a large, black arrow pointing left greeted the pair when they unloaded from the lift. Godric followed the sign to access The Fourth Seraph in the next leg of their journey. Reeves called from behind, cautioning Godric to wait for him. Godric stopped and turned back to his teacher. Reeves stood in the flanks of his poles stuck in the snow. He removed his gloves, and his bare hands lowered, reaching toward his feet. Godric laughed to himself when he saw Reeves's still unbound ski boots. He knew then exactly how much he had to learn. Godric ripped the first run as hard as he could, and Reeves casually bested his student without the need to secure his boots.

Locked into his equipment, he gave Godric instructions for the next run.

"This time, I'll lead. Let me get down to the clearing before you start. I will give a signal when to go. The snow is fresh, so you'll be able to see my tracks clearly. I want you to follow my line and stay inside my line. But also, don't worry about my line."

"I'm confused."

"Do you ever hear people say: 'Be present. Live in the moment?'"

"Sure."

"Well, there's a time and place for that, but it isn't when you're skiing. A skier's mind has to stretch over what's ahead and take action, knowing that *the moment* is just a link between what came before and what is to come. Being present means being reactive by implication. Skiing is a proactive process. Predict. Actualize. Repeat." Reeves said, visibly counting with three fingers in the last sentence.

"On this run, focus on anticipation. Your arms and hands need to be one step ahead to lead your hips and skis. Your mind needs to be three to five steps ahead of that. So follow my line, but never mind where your feet or skis are. You literally can't do anything about where you are at the moment. Always focus on the next turn. The next turn should set you up for the one to follow, and so on. The end of one movement must be the start of the next. So, if you fall off track, ignore where you are. Your next turn—your next set of turns—is where you make the correction and reset your course. Does that make more sense?"

"I understand," Godric said.

"Those racers we just passed—each one of them will memorize a race course and make every move with the entirety of the race in mind."

"That's an interesting strategy."

"It's more than a strategy. Whether on a race course or free skiing in the backcountry, your line— be it chosen or mandated by obstacles—is the primary. It has to underscore every decision you make."

"You're right. That's not a strategy. It's a philosophy."

"Good lord. Do you always look for the philosophy behind everything you're taught?"

"What was it you called skiers and dancers? A herald of beauty? Well, I strive to be a herald of truth. So, yes, I search for the philosophy behind what I am taught, especially the lessons that I find worth following."

"Good," Reeves nodded, accepting the compliment. "Speaking of following, lecture is over. Wait for my signal, and then follow my track. Stay in my line and anticipate!"

Reeves shoved off, leaning into the steep cliff with his arms leading his path. His wrists snapped in successive flicks, tilting forward, while his poles impaled the snow and towed him into every turn. With each move, Reeves' hips sank toward his ankles, and his knees recoiled in succession. He bounced back and forth as if falling along a sinusoidal crack in the mountain and bouncing through it with infinite elasticity. The rapid commotion of his legs clashed with the stillness of his torso, which remained unmoved. Reeves skied as the violent deliverance of a delicate object like a sculpted bust mounted atop a locomotive. The paradox left Godric in wonder over how a man's figure could work with independence, contradict itself, and yet remain an indivisible sum. Godric's sharp mind failed to conjure the words for what he witnessed, so he marked his response as a new emotion—a truth, undoubted and complete unto itself—to be studied and named in self-refection.

Reeves stopped at a flat clearing at the edge of Godric's vision. A cursive path in the snow tethered them together. At the far end, Reeves's hand waved in the air, signaling Godric to start. Godric examined the blueprint he was to trace and, for a moment, questioned his own sanity and the impossibility of his task. It should be simple for a draftsman to trace the work of his master, but Godric scoffed. The path's symmetry and precision seemed manufactured, and its beauty, divine. To mimic it was an act of futility, and marking it with new tracks would constitute defacing a holy epitaph. He reminded himself of what he witnessed: that the line ahead of him was forged by a man on skis, not by a machine on rails nor by the touch of a deity. Godric reminded himself of his long-held belief that one man's achievement is destined to be surpassed by another. Its existence is proof that his task was not futile, and what's more, an attempt to surpass would be a virtue, even if it failed. A spark of conviction swelled in his mind, the combustion of pride and passion—pride over what he witnessed and a passion to eclipse it.

Two sweeping strides sent Godric into the run. He pulled his feet together, looked down, and saw them in the center of Reeves' line. The claustrophobic path left barely enough room for two skis as Godric approached the first turn. His edges bent into the snow, matching the contour and holding Reeves' arc through the turn. The satisfaction of the movement dissipated with the next. Godric sped toward the ensuing waypoint, and his momentum carried him past the mark. He pulled tight in correction. A moment later, Godric's skis reclaimed the center of Reeves' line, and again, he could not hold it. Cutting short on the next turn, Godric tacked back and forth through successive turns, each attempting to compensate for its predecessor and deviating further from the line.

Frustration plagued Godric's technique. The more effort he put to stay the line, the more erratic his path became. Desperation flourishes in the soil of frustration, anger, and embarrassment. Godric grew dejected and cursed himself aloud. He abandoned skiing in Reeves' line and surrendered to his own. He swung away from the path, and the pressure to follow it discharged. In an instant, his instinct to admire the remaining track and the man tied to it returned. As Godric's skis cut his own path, the lesson from his teacher flashed as an aggregate. He forgot where he was, seeing a path pinned between him and Reeves. He set a course, not as individual pivots, but as a long thread of arcs. The peak of one was the start of the next. He set off to follow it, and the farther he mapped the string, the easier it made his skiing. He wove through the connective tissue between his skis and the mountain as if fabricated of his own long-range intention. He still failed to stay within Reeves's line but created his own that matched its spirit. Reeves watched the end of the run, pleased with his student. Godric finished, disappointed in his task but pleased with himself.

Two silhouettes fell as shadows over the clearing as Godric stopped next to Reeves. Reeves looked back at the two paths left on the mountain while Godric forced his attention forward. Reeves saw the lines intersecting in the snow like two recordings of the same song—one fluid, the other failing to find the proper key and tempo until the bridge. Reeves swung his arm, nudging Godric's shoulder and directing his focus to review his performance.

"You struggled at the start, but it looks like you found some rhythm at mid-run." Reeves said with a raised pole pointed at the tracks behind them.

"I'd rather not dwell on it. Let's just move on." Godric replied.

"That's no way to learn," Reeves said.

A scale's balance sways under the stress of a new measurement, and Reeves could see Godric's shoulders gauge the weight of his curiosity against his reluctance. Godric lifted his goggles and turned to view the mess he spewed over Reeves' immaculate lines.

"It's uglier than I thought," Godric said.

"You're a studied man, are you not? A student in practice if not by enrollment?" Reeves asked.

"I try to be," Godric said.

"And you read a lot of books?"

"A few every week. What's your point?"

"When you read a book—one on a particularly challenging subject—what do the pages look like when you're done?"

"They're marked with my notes."

"Predictable. I imagine they're filled with highlighted passages, underlined paragraphs, and circled words. You probably leave comments stricken over the margins on every page."

"I do."

"Do you see those notes as marks of your own

failure to understand the text?"

"No. That's how I understand it."

"Then look back at the tracks and see it the same way. There are parallels between learning a subject and mastering a skill. You compare your tracks and mine and see your failure. I say that failure is a process of mastery."

Sunlight sifted through the churning clouds, exposing the shimmering specks of snow adrift in the air. Godric went mute, still facing the run and offering no reaction to the lesson, while Reeves' eyes rested, watching the flurry float around his quiet student. The silence left Reeves half-expecting to hear the patting of flakes landing on the ground. He waited, giving his student time to process what he heard and saw. Godric gave no attention to the passing time. He did not notice the silence, nor would he have noticed if a cascade of noise rumbled around them. Godric's mind fell into an ingrained pathway of study, leaving him almost catatonic in thought. Only Godric's eyes moved, steering over the slope as if reading and marking a passage to be referenced later with the intention to be preserved as a permanent memory.

It's appropriate that skiing is taught in lessons, Reeves thought as he patiently waited for the most satisfying moment of his job. To be taught a lesson implies the passage of knowledge, skills, and values with the context of their consequences. Reeves coached skiing in the manner of a mentor or parent, not to instill mere proficiency but as a passing of wisdom. Reeves could not hold back his smile when Godric nodded his head. A nod says so much: to accept, to acknowledge, to agree. What more apt gesture to mark the understanding of a lesson than a nod? Reeves knew his teaching was successful. Godric pulled his goggles over his eyes and rocked in his equipment. His knees swayed, but his ankles remained locked inside the rigid shells of his boots. His skis veered from edge to edge as if responding to the neurons meant for his feet and carrying out the command on their behalf. Godric felt comfort seeing his will reflected in his equipment and his immutable connection to it. Reeves watched Godric's attention shift from the lesson to himself and took the cue to continue their day.

"You lead the rest of the way," Reeves said. "Go straight down and keep riding until you reach the flat landing with an old two-seat lift on your right. That's our ticket to Offering Bowl access. Just ski. No instructions or lessons. Find your own line and go. I'll stay behind you."

The unblemished expanse opened before Godric with no plot to follow nor any obstacles to avoid. Liberty is a measure of a man's ability to be candid, daring, and brave, and Godric felt its gravity more than the mountain's. He surrendered and let it serve as his guide. He accelerated, and his speed grew with a yearning to recapture the closing rhythm of his last run. His hands dictated the tempo, and his skis found a natural progression between each beat. He looped through the sequence and let it wash over him like a song with an infectious refrain. He skied the wide-open path, reciting the same movement over and over. The freedom to move left him captivated in motion. He adopted it as a mantra, as if the movement gave name to his own personal resonance.

In clearing above, Reeves delayed his descent, allowing Godric to build a generous separation between them. When Reeves dropped in, he stretched a long line along the boundary, remaining far from Godric's periphery and allowing his student to ski freely. Reeves kept a slow pace, rationing his attention to Godric. He saw his student's hands profess each change in direction the moment before his course altered. And as Godric moved back and forth in a repeating pattern in the snow, it was clear to Reeves that Godric altered nothing and followed an indivisible trajectory set by an internal compass. It led him with both prophecy and commandment as if he chased an invisible shadow cast before him by his own conscious. Still, the snow remained clear before Godric, and he swept through with the fidelity of a photon traversing its own intransigent wave. A continuous contrail streamed from the base of Godric's skis, spraying snow in unique phases, each phase an unalienable evolution to the next. Reeves recognized his coaching in action, seeing Godric project his next three maneuvers in each movement of his hands. Reeves swelled with the compounding pride of a teacher when a student demonstrates a lesson well-taught.

Godric waited for Reeves under the bullwheel of an old chairlift christened Double Barrel. The chairs shivered as they rounded the track to pick up riders, who waited under the rickety creaks groaned by the vintage lift. Godric imagined the noise was an echo from the past carried through all its years of service. Machinery creaks in the same manner as the joints of elderly men. As he waited, Godric rolled his hand in and pulled it to his shoulder in response to what he heard. He thought of his own joints, with their long, smooth motion, and how they would never learn the pain and stiffness that come with that kind of age. He felt the clean rotation of his shoulder and the tendons contacting beneath his forearm, pliable and strong. He remembered the permanent mark it carried, the script from the epic myth that brought him to dream after two sleepless nights. He remembered writing the words in his journal, the pen shaking in his hand, trembling from the rush of adrenaline, the sleepless exhaustion, and the diagnosis weighing on his conscience. He preached the words to himself every day as a motivation, an inspiration, and a dare to wake up and live—just like the young hero, a warrior who wandered the land, keeping an oath to honor a people who no longer existed in his world. He looked at his arm and silently recited the words hidden under the bright orange cover.

Woe be the immortal youth, destined to suffer the consequence of age.

Blessed be a young mortality, beknownst only the rapture of life.

The chairs swung through the loading zone, one after another, ticking through their path with the assurance and fidelity of the hands on a fine-crafted grandfather clock. With its slow, predictable tempo, the chairs rocked, filling the quiet with a chorus of diffused white noise. The sound soothed Godric while waiting for Reeves as he reminded himself that he would not share the old lift's fate.

Reeves slid in behind Godric, and the lift operator nodded them to the next chair. All other lifts on the mountain carried passengers like an escalator, but Double Barrel, the mountain's oldest lift, climbed like a rope ladder. The stiff seat and meager frame of the two-man lift felt like the skeletal remains of a once prosperous lift that left riders fully exposed to its height. Reeves' instincts reached for a safety bar and grasped at the side rails, but he knew neither was there. He pressed his lumbar into the seat corner with the mass of his body and weight of his fear. With two long breaths, he sank further into the point, which offered no refuge from the height.

After a short ascent, the ride delved over a deep ravine. With no ground below and no mountain face ahead, the ride suspended its riders in mid-air. Godric admired the view as they floated through the open space of the gorge but heard Reeves's continued sighs.

"That last run felt good," Godric said, offering Reeves a distraction from the height.

"You found both ends of the spectrum since our last ride," Reeves observed.

"I know. A lot of frustration followed by some satisfaction."

"That's not quite what I mean."

"Okay. Explain."

"Every run is a revolution. The mountain dictates your path. It's lined with boundaries and obstacles: trees, moguls, racing gates, or a trail left by your instructor to follow. Skiing is a revolt against those dictates—to find freedom … No, to create freedom within those confines. Sometimes, the dictates are few and simple, like your last run. On the most difficult runs, they're not. The best skiers—and the most satisfying skiing—exercise autonomy and command the mountain, even amidst the most unforgiving terrain. It's easy to ski free in an open and flat run, but to impose your freedom even in the most restrictive terrain…it's what the great skiers seek. I don't have the word for that."

"Enlightened," Godric stated as a matter of fact.

"You might be the only person who might use that word. Most would call it crazy," Reeves said with a laugh of irony.

"I have learned, even at my young age, that an action's value—its merit—is as much a product of the context and its immediate opportunity as it is of the action itself. Think about a steel beam lying on the ground. It's simple to walk across. You could probably sprint over it or even do a cartwheel on it. Now raise that to the height of a balance beam or to the highest floor of a skyscraper under construction," Godric said, pausing on the last line, remembering their own context. "Sorry," he added.

"Forget it. It helped make your point. And how did you learn this lesson?"

"I was a good athlete in high school. I played a few sports. My favorite was basketball. In my senior year, we won our region. It was historic, at least for our school. We never made it that far in the tournament, let alone won it. I was good, not tall or athletic enough to play in college, but I had skill. At one point during the season, I didn't miss a shot for five straight games. Now, I was selective and only took a few shots per game, but I made them all. Every free throw, too. I was perfect. That's what they said."

"That's impressive."

"I know. I thought so, too. But no one remembers that. The only thing anyone remembers is the game-winning shot my teammate made in the regional final—the local paper dubbed it 'The Miracle Shot' in its headlines. You see, no one shoots buckets in his driveway, dreaming about making every shot in five straight regular season games. It's always a countdown: five … four … three … two … one … 'And the crowd goes wild!'" Godric said, mimicking a basketball shot and holding his hand up at the end of the countdown.

"It's weird," Reeves said. "You're describing winning a championship, and here I feel like I should be offering you my sympathies."

"A couple of years ago, I would have accepted your sympathy. I would have demanded it in a way. You see, this is the lesson I learned because, for a long time, I was resentful of my teammate's miracle shot. I thought that my perfection was superior."

"Isn't it?"

"They say, 'perfection is the enemy of good,' but in reality, it's two different things. Perfection is independent of context. A figure skater can be perfect in practice, but if she always falls in competition, she's mediocre."

"What changed your mind about your teammate?"

"Reflection. Perspective. All of time's remedies. Growing up, I was that kid counting down in his driveway, daydreaming about making a last-second shot in a championship game. A few years passed, and I realized that I was grateful to witness my teammate's shot. I got to see greatness, the dream come to life, the miraculous with my own eyes."

"You sound like the enlightened one."

"Maybe, but that's not quite the enlightenment I was talking about. You described skiers seeking the most difficult terrain. Those skiers understand that context matters, that opportunity matters. They know that performance is one part action and one part what is at stake. I say those skiers are enlightened because they're daring to create context. They're chasing opportunity. They're setting the stakes."

"That's true, but the vast majority aren't skiing in a competition. Hell, many ski alone and would never boast about their triumphs or sulk to others over their failures. They just love *doing* skiing. There's nothing on the line for them."

"Isn't there? I bet they would never be satisfied running blue cruisers all day. They want the novelty, the new landmarks. They want to commandeer the impossible and reclaim it in the name of what's possible. To make the impossible possible. A miracle. That's the opportunity they're chasing. The consequences they face are more dire than a lost competition. They're risking their own hope, living with the knowledge of their own limitation, and perhaps, dying with it."

Can you live with that? The shared thought flowered in both their minds as if the conversation planted the same seed in both Godric and Reeves. Neither said a word nor noticed the quiet. Stillness is a gesture that invites silence, and silence ignites reflection. Each answered, *No,* to the shared thought, but both quickly succumbed to their own futility. Neither saw a choice nor a just action to make amends. Godric slowed his breath, fighting to suppress the memory of what was being taken from him. Reeves' eyes glazed, and his head drooped, accepting remorse as a just punishment for what he took from the young men a day earlier.

The lift broached the final lift tower. Reeves, preoccupied with his own thoughts, did not move. Godric gave him a gentle push with his elbow and readied to unload from the lift.

"Tips up," Godric said after the nudge as he nodded and read the words on the tower's warning sign.

The pair jettisoned the chairlift, and habit took over for Reeves as he slid down the ramp. Routines beget action without thought, the acquired instincts from a thousand repetitions of a task. The surroundings triggered the reflex in Reeves. The shadows of the tree line, the small ski patrol hut, and the shape of the sky painted a star on the mountain mapped in Reeves' mind with the thought: *you are here.*

A group of skiers surrounded a large trail map next to the ski patrol hut. They pointed and gestured with their poles, deliberating on a path. Reeves led Godric past them, following the clear course in his mind. Godric kept Reeves' side, and the duo skated until they reached a rounded ridge.

The ridge bowed to the northeast. Vertical lines engrossed the steep slope, cutting the snow with long chords that pointed to a single point at the bottom of the curved run. The slope's grooming was sublime, and its steep pitch stood like an Arcadian paradise, ripe for any skier wishing to exert control over speed. A mountain taunts skiers in many ways. Godric has heard its twisted persuasion on the most challenging runs, as if the mountain dares, "You can't." Hovering over the crescent ridge, he distinctly heard the mountain whisper, "Do whatever you'd like."

The temptation brought Godric to a stop. He paused, admiring the run. The corduroy lines stretched across the frame of the straight boundary below him and an arching shadow far across the northeast side. If the crescent ridge were a canvas then the image below was the painting of a concert harp, begging to be played. Godric turned his skis parallel with the slope and prepared to slide down, ignoring his teacher's lead.

"I wouldn't," Reeves called out when he lost sight of his student.

"It's so perfect," Godric said with a sigh.

"No." Reeves said in a stern command.

Within a moment, Reeves stood next to his student. In his speed, Godric could not distinguish Reeves's sharp pivot from the bounding shuffle back up the ridge. Godric found himself stuck in his teacher's gate. Reeves' stiff arm raised across Godric's chest, and Godric felt the pressure from Reeves's warning against his ribs.

"Why?" Godric huffed.

"The conditions aren't what they look like. You'll regret it, and once you're in, there's no way out." Reeves said.

"Better tell her," Godric said, pointing at a skier in a white coat halfway up the ridge.

As Godric raised his pole toward the skier, she dropped into the run. The flash of lightning precedes the boom of thunder, but Godric could hear the danger before the woman saw it. Her skis clapped against the hard, uneven ground. Icy teeth in the slope's rigid lines snapped at her skis. They reverberated in response to the violence, and the flex that had once pressed the edges into the snow for control now recoiled in chaos. She moved to stop, but the hard, serrated ice provided nothing to grip. Her hip hit the ground first, followed by her knee and ribs. Her elbow bounced as momentum dragged her body over the sharp, coarse grain of the surface. A line of pain swelled and contracted from her shin to her shoulder, throbbing under the insulation of her clothes, which could not protect her from the abrasions. Futile tears dripped under her cries, and the salty drops froze when they hit the jagged ice.

"She's in trouble," Godric said.

"The slope is like a grinder made of ice. The sun baked it the other day, and then the temperature crashed, hardening it like this. It's unskiable."

The woman stood for another attempt. They watched as she struggled to move even a few feet before crashing again. The cold and thin air diluted her cries. Godric and Reeves were the only people on the mountain who noticed her. She raised her hands and levered herself up with her poles. She stood for a moment—her courage exhausted and paralyzed in fear—then collapsed in panic.

"She needs help. Can you radio ski patrol?" Godric said.

"No," Reeves said in a pointed voice. "That's not what she needs."

Reeves strapped his poles to his wrists and pulled his goggles over his eyes. The swift moves assured Godric that whatever would happen next was under Reeves' control.

"Go to the far end of the ridge and ski down. Stick to the shaded area of this run, and you'll be okay. The snow is still soft in the shade. Go to the lift at the bottom. Wait for me, and I will meet you there.

Godric watched Reeves damn hesitation. Reeves did not slide into the hill with caution; he jumped into the air and attacked it. His feet hit the ground as if targeting a landmine, and he exploded with a vault to make his turn in the air instead of on the snow. Then Reeves, the artisan, became a butcher. He cleaved the ice with his skis, scoring its surface with a trail of disconnected vees. Ice shavings sprayed out as he pounced from stroke to stroke, leaving a frozen wake spanning the edge of the ridge toward the woman who collapsed on the ice. The sweeping gashes defiled the slope's pristine façade at first glance, but under inspection, the bare patches of ice revealed its true nature. At its end, Reeves braked with a punishing stop that landed like a slap and scolded the mountain face.

The woman made no calls for help; the unscalable run convinced her that help was not possible. She lay in discomfort on the jagged ice, choosing to endure the pain of the slope's harrowing thorns over another attempt to ski it. For a moment, the world offered nothing except a prison of her own despair. Her eyes did not catch Reeves inching up the hill toward her. He crept slowly as one would approach a wounded animal, unsure if she would rejoice or snap.

"Are you hurt?" Reeves asked.

"I'm not sure," the woman said, certain of nothing.

"I saw you standing a minute ago. Can you get up again?"

"It's too hard. I can't. I can't," the woman whimpered between gasps of breath.

"Do you want to get down this mountain?"

"Yes," she said behind tears.

"Then eyes up here," Reeves said in a voice that demanded obedience over emotion. The woman's eyes met Reeves'. The first drops of confidence spilled on her from the sight of Reeves' composure.

"My name is Zack. I'm a ski instructor. I'm going to show you how to get down this hill, but I need you to listen closely and do everything I say. Can you do that?"

"I don't know," the woman said in a shaking voice.

"The answer is 'yes,'" Reeves said, not permitting any doubt from the woman. "Now, can you do that?" he asked again.

"Yes," she answered, steadied by Reeves' conviction.

"Good. What's your name?"

"Kayia."

"Nice to meet you, Kayia. First, I need you to stand up. I know you can do it because I saw you on your feet just before I got here. Get up just like you did before—it was perfect. Dig your poles in the ground. Keep your left pole upslope and the other downslope below your right ski. Like this," Reeves said, demonstrating his instructions.

"First thing: press your feet into the ground and push up with your right arm at the same time. Then, when you start to rise, pull with your left arm. It will give you more leverage to stand and balance," he added.

The gaskets stretched over the ice. Kayia stabbed the snow with all her strength, and her arms hung like cross-beams from the pillars of her two poles. She wanted to rise, but fraught fear blocked the command she sent to her limbs. She did not move and remained in her set position, failing to launch.

Reeves waited with patience. Then, he spoke with patience.

"Does it hurt?" Reeves asked.

"No. I just … I can't do it," Kayia said.

"Yes, you can do this. First, I want you to take a deep breath. Get a slow inhale until your lungs stretch. Then breathe out all the air all at once … Good. Perfect. Now, do that two more times … Now, don't try to stand, but flex the top and back of your thighs. Contract. Pull them tight. Do you feel the tension?"

"Yes."

"Now harden your tummy and get your back stiff."

Reeves watched as Kayia's spine straightened and her weight loaded over her hips.

"Now! Press-up! Drive your feet through your skis. Drive! Drive! Drive! Drive!"

Kayia catapulted to her feet. Her shadow left a void that erased the ice beneath her. She stood tall and stable over the void, keeping all the sunlight for herself. Heat radiated from her core as warm blood tingled through her limbs. The warmth washed over her pain. She looked to Reeves. He saw the tear marks over her cheeks, contradicting the new determination across her face. Kayia spoke no words but held a new temper that implored Reeves for more.

"This is where it gets scary, but courage requires fear. So be brave when you do this. I want you to lead with your heels. Shift your weight back and move backward across the slope."

Kayia followed the instructions, treading a few inches over the hostile ground.

"Push your hips back toward your heels. Good!" Reeves said. "Now shift your weight back to center," he added as Kayia slowed to a stop.

"Kayia, that's it. You have the hang of it. Now, as soon as you start to move, lean hard on your inside edges. You'll get traction, just enough to set your direction. Keep the pressure on your edge, and you'll turn. Keep turning until your skis get the downslope. As soon as your momentum stops, lean forward, and you'll start to move down. Don't be afraid; hold that edge. You'll keep turning until your heels point downhill again. Then, repeat the whole process. Like this."

Reeves gave another demonstration of the action. His skis skittered backward, rattling over the ice. The arced path solved the problem of speed. Gravity started Reeves down, then across the slope, and finished with a natural break as his momentum turned his back uphill. He slowed, paused, and then started another arc, this time moving forward. Once again, he slid down, grating his skis against the ice, and then gravity slowed him to a halt as he turned upslope.

"That's what I want you to do. Just swing back and forth. Start backward until you feel a downward pull, then lean forward, but always press the inside of your skis."

Kayia slid backward again to a stop. Reeves reinforced his instruction. She leaned forward, almost falling, but Reeves' directions held her up. She kept her weight on the edge of her skis. She turned uphill, centered herself, and came to a gentle stop.

"Yes! That's it!" Reeves shouted. "Now again. Back and forth. Take your time. Stop as often as you need to catch your breath or get your balance."

At the top of the Ridge, Godric did not move. He stood frozen at first in concern over the fallen women, then in awe over his teacher's exploits. Awe vanquished concern. Godric admired Reeves skiing over the treacherous as an exhibit of mastery and his teaching of Kayia, its pinnacle. What Reeves said and showed to Kayia armed her with the technique and the courage to battle her own way down the cold, hard grit. As Reeves led Kayia down the ice, Godric left to follow the softer, shadowed path to the base.

Kayia drifted to and fro. At first, she stopped frequently. As her comfort grew, she stitched a string of maneuvers together. Then another. And another. Each added a leg to the one preceding it. Her heavy lungs lightened with each stop. She dispelled her panic as if she breathed fresh confidence and exhaled despair. Still, the journey down remained tenuous. Kayia repeated the procedure as if running a drill that offered her no comfort or joy. It did, however, offer progress. What Reeves taught her only neutralized the threat of the slope but did not bring mastery or even competence. It was only a way down. She fluttered, following Reeves' instructions for over fifteen minutes until the slope flattened, and Reeves signaled her to stop.

Reeves stepped out of his bindings and invited Kayia to do the same. Reeves collected Kayla's skis and mounted them upon his shoulder, across from his own. Reeves hiked along the weakened descent, and Kayia kept pace next to him. The sound of shattering ice cracked with each step, and Kayia felt the shards crumble to dust under her feet.

"You did good," Reeves said. It was his first words to her that did not sound like an order from a commanding officer. He resisted the urge to ask if she was okay.

"I thought," she said, letting out a laugh of relief, "they'll have to send a helicopter to get me. I owe … just … Zack, thank you."

"You handled it. That was the toughest run on the mountain. You skied that. You can ski anything and never have to think about helicopters."

"Really? The toughest?" Kayia challenged.

"The toughest. You can ski snow and smooth ice. Ice is not ideal, but you can scrape your way along. Rigid, uneven ice on a pitch as steep as this makes skiing impossible. But you did it. You can handle anything now."

"I doubt that."

"What you just learned can scale any run on the mountain."

"Back-and-forth. Slow. Work the inside edge," Kayia said, repeating the lesson to set in her memory.

"It's called the *Falling Leaf.* If you find yourself in trouble again, gently float your way down just like a leaf breaking off a tree in the late autumn. You'll be fine."

Near the lift lanes, Reeves felt Kayia moving in for an embrace. He let her skis slip down from his shoulder to land as a post between them. He separated and laid them on the ground for her to remount and move on with her day. In two steps, she was back in her skis. Kayia pulled out her phone to check her messages."

"Do you know how to get to South Paw Slider?" Kayia said.

"Take this lift and keep left after you unload. You can't miss it. Have a group waiting for you?" Reeves said.

"Family."

"How long are you here for?"

"We're skiing today and tomorrow and leave the next morning."

"Time's running out. You better go catch up with your family."

"Yes. I'm … I don't know what to say except thank you, Zack."

"Just enjoy the rest of your trip."

"I will."

"So long, Kayia."

"So long."

Kayia shoved her poles into the ground and made two long kicks that carried her to the loading zone. Lanes on either side of the lift merged where Kayia caught a chair, carrying her up and out of sight. Across the intersection, Godric leaned forward, letting his poles brace his weight while he kept his left ear pointed toward Reeves. Godric rested, not noticing that over a dozen chairs passed before Reeves dropped his own skis onto the ground and locked into his bindings. The snap of the skis landing on the snow sprung Godric to attention. Godric's hips thrust upward. His shoulders pulled back, and he slid forward—reaction opposed action in observance of Newton's third law.

The safety bar closed over Reeves and Godric, and the chair accelerated up the line toward the north end of The Fourth Seraph. Reeves pulled his boots onto the footrest and locked his elbow around the hanger. Godric gave one last exam of the hillside and the scars that Reeves left on the ice.

"What's that run called?" Godric asked.

"Devil'd Eggs." Reeves said.

"You said it was unskiable."

"I wouldn't call what she did skiing."

"I'd call that skiing" Godric said, pointing to Reeves's tracks in the ice but thinking of the forbidden path on the backside of the mountain.

"That wasn't skiing; that was only doing what's necessary."

"Speaking of necessary, I'm curious. When I suggested calling ski patrol, you said, 'That's not what she needs.' What did you mean by that?"

"How was she when we first saw her fall?"

"She was terrified."

"And what is she doing now?"

"I imagine getting off this lift and trying to meet up with her family."

"Exactly. She's moving on. If I called ski patrol, they would have lowered her down the hill with ropes and a sled. They would have pulled her off the mountain for a medical check-up, which is standard procedure, liability and all. She wouldn't get back on the slopes today or tomorrow. Perhaps never again. Now, she's riding up the lift alone with a new knowledge that she can handle any run on the mountain. She has a tool that she did not have when she fell. Life for her is less scary. What was a trauma is now a strength. If I called ski patrol, that trauma becomes more permanent."

"What you taught her, The Falling Leaf, can it really be used to ski any terrain?"

"Yes. She'll be able to use it to slip out of any trouble she finds on this mountain."

"Then why can't someone use it to ski *The Falls*?" Godric said, his mind revisiting the bookmark he placed on their first gondola ride.

"Ah! So *that's* where you were going with this cross-exam? I'm not going to plant any seeds for you to test *The Falls*."

"This isn't about *The Falls*. It's a serious question about The Falling Leaf. You said it can be used to ski any run on the mountain. Well, why not *The Falls*?" Godric deflected.

"The terrain won't allow it."

"How can you know that if no one has ever seen it?"

"I have seen it."

"How, if access to it from below is restricted?"

"A few years ago, during spring skiing, I hiked out Two-and-Half Pass. I packed a drone and flew it off the edge of Hallow's Gallows. After a few hundred feet or so of snow cover, the backside is nothing but exposed rock face. Nothing but straight vertical rock."

"That's so strange for nothing to be skiable on the

backside there, given how famous the rest of the topography is back there. From everything I have read about this mountain, the north and south bowls on the backside are renowned by skiers. I remember reading one review that said, 'I hold a hope that, when I die, I find mountains in heaven. But I hold no illusions that skiing in paradise will be as good as what I found in deep bowls behind The Seraphs.' That description is what compelled me to visit."

"That's not *The Falls*, unfortunately. I did see one line with potential. There was a patchwork of snow running down a vertical ridge. The ridge was narrow and terrifyingly steep, but it had enough of a pitch to hold a patchwork of snow even into March. With the right conditions, it's possible that it could catch a snowfall from top-to-bottom."

"So why not Falling Leaf down that ridge."

"Because death. The Falling Leaf avoids the fall line. The ridge I saw would force you to embrace it. Even with complete snow cover, the ridge is so narrow and steep that there's no choice but to ski back and forth over its peak. Even then, you have to maintain perfect control and make perfect turns. If you go too fast, the ridge will act like a ramp that will launch you off the mountain with nowhere to land. If you go too slow, you'll slip right off the mountain face. To even have a chance, it would take the perfect skier in the perfect conditions."

"Perfect conditions? Like now?"

"Now you're trying to plant a seed in my head."

"You took a drone to scout the area. I'd say the seed is already there. And blooming."

"I was curious. Seeing the drone footage satisfied my curiosity."

"Now I'm curious. How many times did you have to watch the footage before you were satisfied?" Godric asked.

Reeves did not answer. Godric did not expect an answer. The wind whirred between them, erasing the possibility of silence. Godric turned his gaze over his right shoulder toward The Third Seraph while Reeves replayed the memory of drone footage. Reeves examined the vivid image of the dangerous ridge, while Godric charted a course: Two-and-a-Half Pass, then through Hallow's Gallows. Reeves did not realize the map that he unintentionally gifted to his student. Godric followed the map in his mind and could think of nothing else.

Across the mountain, the flurries thickened, and the queues of skiers grew longer at each chairlift. Visibility waned as snowfall capped the heights of the mountain with the frozen fog of a swelling white-out. Reeves and Godric unloaded on The Fourth Seraph. Godric pressed his neck forward, grasping at every inch of visibility. Skiers crossed in and out of his sight without warning, and Godric slid forward, unsure if he was heading toward the next run or a cliff.

"What's say we break for lunch," Reeves said with the wisdom of twenty years.

"It's a little early."

"Yes. But let's go anyway. Moose Call Lodge is straight ahead. We can wait out this storm and let things clear up a bit. Plus, we'll beat the crowd that will come in at lunchtime. When we head back out, that same crowd will sit in the cafeterias, and traffic in the bowls will thin out."

A fireplace ran along the entirety of the lodge's northern wall. The continuous flames pulsed, sending heat and comfort to nearby diners. In front of the fire, two plastic trays met atop a picnic-style table, forming a sort of chess board between Aris Godric and Zack Reeves. They both sat at attention with their heavy coats hanging on the next chairs, like a pair of spirits joining their meal. Reeves crushed crackers over a large bowl of chili and then blew across the top of his customary hot cocoa. Godric lifted a glass of water behind his unwrapped sandwich. Godric did not feel thirsty until he started drinking the cold liquid, sending sunbursts of a fuel that he did not know he needed. A small sip became a gulp, and a moment later, the glass was empty. Reeves moved his glass of water over to Godric's tray.

"Drink up. You need it."

"What about you?"

"I have everything I need."

Reeves shoveled a spoonful of chili into his mouth, savoring the taste before swallowing. Godric smiled as he noticed Reeves' choice of meal and bet himself that no choice was involved.

"You're a skier to a fault," Godric said, impersonating Chelle's comment at The Steep Easy. "I bet you eat that every single time you're here."

"You're worse than Chelle."

"I guess you are but a creature of habit."

"I'm a creature of routines," Reeves corrected with raised eyebrows.

"What is the difference?"

"Creatures of habit act on inertia. Creatures of routines act with intention."

Godric leaned forward, his forearms at rest on the edge of the table, contemplating Reeves's words. Reeves gathered his thoughts over another bite of his steaming chili.

"Say more," Godric inquired.

"Habits develop out of comfort," Reeves said, expanding his thoughts. "They're orientated toward the past to maintain the status quo. I developed routines oriented toward outcomes and refined them based on new learnings along with my own trial and error. I eat this chili because it's warm, doesn't sit heavy, and has what I need to rejuvenate for the rest of the day. I drink hot cocoa because I enjoy the taste, and it's intertwined with the experience of skiing. It makes it complete, whole. I might as well be sipping serotonin and dopamine because it's like drinking liquid love."

"So is that the secret then?"

"Secret to what?"

"The secret to what you wrote: to make each day better than the one before it; to wake up every morning on the best day of your life."

Reeves's cheeks rose over a bouncing chest as he chuckled at Godric's suggestion. Godric's face kept a stoic demeanor, not letting the question fall unanswered in levity. When opposing dispositions meet, composure acts as a corrective mirror. Reeves' shoulders stiffened, and the amusement unfurled from his smile in response to Godric's devotion to his own curiosity.

"No," Reeves said. "The real secret is finding your loves and connecting everything you do to them."

"You can't do what you love every second of the day."

"Can't you? I am eating a meal right now, but I eat to get energy so that *I may ski*. I go to sleep for the same reason and doze off under the memories and ruminations of skiing the best mountains in the world. So much that the moment I fall asleep feels like that first drop onto a steep run."

"What about the bad days when the conditions are poor, or you have a lesson with a rude customer."

Reeves' eyes locked onto Godric's and directed them to the large window, the white-out beyond the glass barrier, and the piles of snow building on the bottom of the pane.

"Of all days to ask that question."

"Great days happen. So do bad ones."

"True. But you can't live for the exceptions. What kind of life would you have if happiness were only possible a handful of times per year? This weather system we had this year—these conditions—come once a decade if you're lucky."

"So what do you do then?"

"You love the doing. And work to get so good at it that it doesn't matter if you find yourself in fresh powder, or wet slop, or never-ending moguls. No matter what, you can *do the doing* on your terms and in your own way."

"But there is so much that isn't in your control."

"That's true, but you can avoid being overwhelmed by the infinite variables by controlling the finite ones. True, you can't control the conditions or the weather. Nor can you control the actions of others. Or if you get injured or terribly sick."

"Even when you get stuck on a chairlift," Godric interjected, bringing up Reeves' ailment within the thought of his own.

"I didn't know I was that obvious. My clients never notice. Chelle does, every time," Reeves said, gripping his silverware as tight as he held the safety bar on a tall chairlift.

"Do you always get scared when you ride up?"

"I've been a skier for about forty years, and it still terrifies me every single time. But that's part of skiing. Every ride, I have to choose to face the fear or not ski. And that's no choice. So much is out of your hands—in skiing and in life—so control what you can to put yourself in the position to maximize your opportunities and capitalize on them. I've found that when you do that, the opportunities are aplenty."

"What do you do to maximize your opportunities?"

"That goes back to my routines."

"What are they, aside from chili and hot cocoa?"

"There are many. One example is waxing my skis every day, whether they need it or not."

"What good does that do?"

"The simple answer is that it gives me confidence that my equipment is optimized and the trust it will perform. The bigger part is what it does for my mind. I can't explain it, but it's like a chemical reaction. The act of setting up my skis, stripping off the old wax and grime, running my fingers along the base—it connects me with my skis. And then the scent of the melted wax—in a kitchen that would smell old and stale, but in my cold garage, it's serene and warming—sends signals to my brain. The whole process is like a ceremony or a rite of affirmation, and at the end, my entire being knows it's time to ski."

Godric's head bounced in consensus with every phrase Reeves shared. A sentiment of "Yes…Yes… Yes" repeated in his mind as a web of connections flared across Godric's memories. Its thread sprawled across disparate experiences and observations to render the clear drawing of an unnamed truth that he held but never recognized on his own.

"We used to say 'Get your mind right,' on my basketball team. I never thought about it in your terms, but I should have. There are a million things that athletes do for that same purpose. People call it superstition. I had teammates not wash their jerseys after a win, park in the same parking spot on game day, and only have their ankles taped by a specific trainer. Guys will adjust their uniforms in a particular way, eat the same meal, and compulsively organize their locker. No one believes that any of it impacts the game or how they play. Except for music! Oh yes, go into a locker room when a team is getting dressed, and every player has headphones to get excited or focused or whatever mindset they need. Hell, every single player has a meticulous routine they go through every time they shoot a free throw—literally the easiest shot in the game. As I think about what you said, I understand the why. Games are chaotic. There's so much that is out of your control, so people adopt these superstitions because it's something they can control amid that chaos."

"You get it," Reeves said, gently tapping his white styrofoam cup against Godric's water glass in a toast to his student.

"I can see why she likes you."

"Who?"

"The bartender. Chelle."

"Please. She's not interested in me."

"She pulled up that article you wrote like she had it staged in a holster. She's interested."

"No. She's interested in the idea of me, the guy in that article."

"That is you."

"No. That was an impulsive stream of consciousness—just some ideas that poured out of me when I opened a spigot in my mind."

"What are we if not our ideas?"

"We're only our ideas if we put them into action. I haven't."

"Not from what I see."

"You're a smart kid. Read between the lines. Make an inference. If I am being measured by my words, then I'm a fraud who can't live up to them. It's true that every day that I get to challenge, or explore, or guide someone on this mountain is better than the one before it. But I wonder sometimes about the value of chasing something that doesn't exist. Yes, I'm making every day better. I believe there are always ways to improve. Always. A skier can always get better. So, I'm chasing perfection and, at the same time, admitting that perfection doesn't exist. To use your words, I aspire to an impossibility and am in pursuit of a miracle. It's futile by definition. I love every moment, but I will die in that futility. I can't resolve that dilemma."

"I can. It's that enlightenment I talked about earlier. You need the context, the right opportunity. Something that is on the line: something that you value so much, and its very existence depends on you being at your very best."

"If that's true, then what do I do different?"

"Absolutely nothing. You give yourself the best chance every day to be the hero like my teammate and his miracle shot—not everyone gets to be that. But even if it never comes, you'll live a damn good life along the way."

"I want to be the hero. I want resolution."

"Say you do resolve it; what will you do then?"

"You mean if I manifest a miracle?"

"Sure. Call it that."

"Then I'll step out of my skis, plant them in triumph, and finally march as the man I wrote about."

"March where?"

"To see Chelle."

Amen! The word bellowed in Godric's mind. It purged every memory and notion in his immediate conscious, save one: *don't show it.* Godric brought Reeves to the precipice of a truth that he knew would be undermined by saying it outright. He has to realize on his own, Godric thought, that to love someone and to welcome the love of another, he must love himself as prerequisite. He must consecrate himself worthy before accepting life's greatest reward. This is the root of dignity. Without that, man is a cynic who laments love. With it, love is a hymn sung by the soul in the glory of being alive. And Godric knew that such a song cannot be composed for another.

The quiet moments that followed peeled back the blanket of snowfall, dispersing the sunlight through the lodge's grand windows. It was a dull glow—a light without shine—and worked as an inverted spotlight with a polarity that separated marquee from focus. Drawing a curtain in a sunless room plants the urge to look outside, as such, Reeves glanced out the window. The blizzard lifted. The snow continued to fall in a steady but slow cadence. So much that one could pick out a single spec in the sky and follow its sway from its birth to the ground. It revealed the mass of skiers gathering near the lodge entrance, the chairs climbing up the mountainside, and the silhouettes of distant mountain peaks, which the thinning snowfall could no longer hide.

Godric stood to fasten his coat while Reeves cleared the table. Before their seats were empty, a group holding loaded trays waited for the premium spot next to the fire. The queue at the register let a steady flow of hungry skiers into the cafeteria. Reeves and Godric hastened through the growing stream as if each person were the pulse of a beacon inviting them back to the mountain. Blue led orange through the irruption of people, forging through the traffic into the open air. Cold splashed against their faces and dripped into every open seam. Godric felt his skin tighten in response, and the tingling of his own invigorating energy spread like a shell over his body. For Reeves, the air fanned the ember in his chest, his ribs, the grates of an inferno that powered his being.

Part Four: *The Aesthetes*

The edge of Offering Bowl could not be traced by a skier's eyes. Its name was apropos of its gift: intimate confines amid an infinite expanse. Its topography broke the valley into distinct sections with natural barriers between them, so that at any point, a skier could only see the slope immediately below him and an apex across the gorge, composed of two ridge lines that seem to narrow but never meet. Its oblong shape skewed the perspective, giving the impression that, should one explore the far edge, he would discover that the more he traveled toward it, the farther away it would get.

Reeves and Godric took no pause until they reached the bowl's edge. Their blue and orange coats flew as an airborne torch, landing gently atop Offering Bowl as if it were both their target and zenith. Many skiers took runs in the bowl, but the snowstorm purged any evidence. Godric pointed his skis toward the cliff's brow and felt surrounded by infinities: the bowl's ever-reaching edge, the eternal sky above, and a perpetual snowfall that left the ground hollow. He admired the falling crystals and rich luxury of the slope's shimmering glaze. Reeves lagged behind, ceding an unnecessary distance between them as if to say: this moment is yours.

"I am almost afraid to speak; it's like I should only whisper," Godric said, spellbound by the awe of the surroundings.

"This is a cathedral," Reeves said, affirming Godric's reverence for the terrain. "Skiers consider this holy ground and make pilgrimage to ski here on a day like today."

"Any instructions?"

"Not right now. You can pretty much make your own line. All the obstacles are buried deep in the snow base."

"Except for those shrubs there," Godric said, pointing at the sporadic branches of short green bristles sprouting from the snow.

Reeves bent over in uncontrollable laughter. His stomach seized, pulling in toward his spine as he fell over his poles. Confused and curious, Godric opened his arms and raised his hands in a plea for explanation. Reeves tried to respond, but each time he formed an answer, he collapsed into a cycle of hysteria. The word punchline had never been more appropriate.

"What?" Godric demanded. He shoved his poles deep into the soft snow, and Reeves recovered his composure.

"Those aren't bushes," Reeves explained. "They're the tips of thirty-foot trees. That's how much snow is beneath you right now. A month ago, this was a wooded grove. Today, it's all open glades."

A pair of straight grooves burrowed into the white bank beneath Godric's feet. He hovered in stasis at the edge of the bowl, gliding his skis to test the depth of the base. He slipped down an inch, then three, until he could no longer see the top of his boots. The snow kept parting, and he thought for a moment that he could sever his way through the whole of the Earth. Godric made two hard stomps in a stationary march, repacking the grooves into a stable platform. His legs coiled and loaded, pressing into compacted firn beneath the soles of his feet. With outstretched hands, his poles primed his body, gathering tension for imminent release.

"May I?" Godric asked permission as a formality. His goggles hugged his cheeks as he squeezed his palms against the handles of his poles.

"It's all yours." Reeves said.

The shriek of exhalation followed Godric as he launched into the air. The upper rim carried the elated howl across the gorge, filling the valley with echos of his excitement. White silk spired in every direction as Godric's violent leap landed with a soft thud in the deep powder. His orange coat burst from the flying debris with a surge that thrust him from the trough of his impact crater.

At once, Godric thought he skied through a mirage. He cut through the slope's ethereal surface, but the mountain provided no base for his blades to carve. His skis wavered through the endless heaps of white silt, unable to sustain a straight track. The intangible sediment pulled Godric deeper as if he were skiing through frosted quicksand. He fought the tongue of the mountain as it tried to swallow him whole. He shifted his weight to his heels, raising the tips of his skis toward the sky. He planed out of the closing mouth behind him only to clash against the viscosity of the dense, crystalline ash parting between his skis.

Control eluded him, and Godric became desperate to regain it. His legs swung wide in his first turn, pressing outward, farther and farther, in search of a base that did not exist. The mountain withdrew its resistance, and Godric moved to strike what was now an apparition. The whole of his strength stretched from his scapula through his feet, expecting the mountain to recoil in turn. His effort was forfeit against the mountain's indifferent neutrality. Godric's skis charged past their mark, and his outstretched limbs left him without recourse. He felt his body go parallel with the slope, flying weightlessly through the particle fog. He reached to brace his fall, and the powder grabbed his arm, torquing his body into a tumble. The mountain was as stern as it was compassionate. The snow ripped his left ski from its binding but cushioned Godric's fall as he rolled through the plow. Godric sprang upright and wiped the mess from the lens of his goggles before Reeves could shout in concern.

Reeves dropped, making bounding maneuvers that brought him to a stop thirty feet above Godric. The long planks inched over the gaping imprint left by Godric's fall. They plowed the mounds with short, careful strokes, scouring the covered mass for Godric's lost ski. Reeves probed the slope with his poles, making deep, penetrating stabs, thrusting until his hand disappeared into the flesh of the snow. Godric made futile attempts to climb toward Reeves, picking at the ground with his poles and stepping with his ski and naked boot. With each upward move, the mountain collapsed, and Godric slipped farther down the pitch. Unable to climb, Godric anchored himself in place and began to fear that his ski was forever lost in the snowy abyss. He examined the stability of his remaining ski with thoughts of the para-skier he witnessed racing in his mind, and Godric questioned his ability to navigate the slope with one ski.

Reeves continued hunting in Godric's fall zone until he felt the basket of his ski pole hook a solid object buried in the snow. He poked the ground in successive repetitions, outlining the ski's position with the hard knocks of cold steel pounding against hardened polymer. He exposed the back edge of the ski and pried it out of the chalky depths. Reeves floated down the mountainside, with Godric's lost ski resting across the mantle of his shoulder blades. The wake left a fresh layer of dust on Godric's side as Reeves braked at his feet. Reeves shoveled a long shelf from the snow next to Godric's boot and placed the ski upon it. Reeves braced the ski, shoving his poles underneath it as a set of girders, and when Godric stepped in, Reeves locked the binding by hand, knowing that the mountain would not grant necessary leverage for Godric to mount them on his own.

"Thank you," Godric said in recognition and deep appreciation for his instructor's experience.

"You're good," Reeves said, brushing the snow from the binding to inspect the toe and heel pieces.

"For a minute there, I thought I'd have to find my way down on a single ski," Godric confessed.

"It's possible. Amputees and monoskiers do it."

"I know. I saw one racing earlier. Makes me look foolish. I'm not good enough to ski this on a pair, let alone one."

"Yes, you are. I would not have brought you here otherwise."

"How do I do it?" Godric asked, his voice carrying the strength and implicit confidence of his teacher's answer.

"It's all about balance. The snow is billowy, so you have to ride on top of it. Squeeze your thighs. That will keep your skis together so they act as a single plane. The more surface area you create, the more the snow will lift you. But you must keep your speed and point your tips out of the crud to generate lift to keep you afloat."

"I felt that, but when I tried, I felt resistance from the snow."

"Right. It's tricky. You have to center on two points," Reeve said as his hands swiped across at the air and then down in the shape of a cross. "Keep your horizontal center squared where your heel and midfoot meet. On the vertical, press right just beyond your tipping point."

"How do I know my tipping point?"

"Good question. Imagine you're standing straight on barefoot flat ground. Then you lean forward an inch. Then, an inch more. Keep leaning until you hit the point where you have to step forward to catch yourself falling. That moment is your tipping point."

"So, to keep my balance, I need to fall."

"That's all skiing is, a controlled fall."

"Sounds more like flying."

"Doesn't it? Generations of men watched in envy as birds soared above in the open air without machines. We wrote myths like that of Icarus and supermen. Then we discovered skiing. Skiers who know have no envy of birds."

"I guess it's fitting that we spread melted wax on our skis."

"You are learning," Reeves said with pride in learning from his student's own revelation. "Imagine your tipping point as a solid plane in front of you. Lean into it so your forehead presses against it at all times. That will help keep you plowing through when the powder pushes back."

"If I'm always falling, how do I control my speed?"

"Through your turns," Reeves answered.

"That's how I wiped out."

"You wiped out because you overstretched, expecting the mountain to catch you like a packed run. That works on piste. It won't here. Don't press into your turns. Collapse down. Compress to lower your center of gravity. Rotate your hips, keeping tight through your legs like there's an axle rod that connects your pelvis to your feet. Turn your hips to pivot your ankles. Then, lift up toward the sky, and you will glide in and out of your turns without the need to press down. Keep your skis together so the powder can raise you like air lifting the wings of an airplane. You won't break like on a groomer, but the angles will absorb your momentum. Gravity will serve to slow your vertical speed. Physics is your ally; that's your control.

"But again, there's a balance," Reeves added a caveat. "Don't over turn. The powder is so thick that if you stray too far from the fall line, you'll slow down too much, and the snow will coagulate in front of you. You'll crash into a wall of your own making. To ski here, you have to ignore any fear and eliminate hesitation. You have to commit to the fall line."

"There's that term again. What's the fall line?"

"It's the straight line from wherever you are on a slope to the base of the mountain. We turn in arcs, and as our skis run along that arc, around the peak of the curve, we are pointing straight down to the bottom. That's where you'll get the most power and speed. Stray too far from it, and you won't be able to plow through the thick powder. Stay on it too long, and you'll speed beyond your control."

"Just like Icarus," Godric said.

"Not quite. Remember, Icarus was the one who fell to the Aegean Sea."

The lesson splashed over Godric, seeping into the open pores of his mind. Godric mimicked the instructions as if each call were a tug on the string of a marionette. He tucked, stretched, and shifted his waist, applying the techniques while replaying the flashback of his fall. He relived the panic of fleeing the gaping jaws of snow that snapped at his heels, grasping for support that did not exist, and meeting his demise against an adversary devoid of both malice and mercy. Each movement was both rehearsal and rendition, reliving what had passed and enacting what was to come—Godric imposed intention upon his memories, armed with a new counter for each failure.

Competence is a product forged in the fires of experience. Practice and failure burn impurities within our knowledge in a progression of answers and questions. Godric's first attempt on Offering Bowl ended as it began: with reckless abandon. His own error left him battered, but even iron must be smelted and hammered to produce steel tools. The precipice atop Offering Bowl offered infinite exhilaration in response to Godric's ever-present question of "Why?" provoking Godric's impulsion. Godric dashed into his second attempt with an answer to the practical question: "How?"

Godric skimmed down the run, fishtailing through his maneuvers but heeding his lessons to keep balanced. His skis slipped often, and he held his first turns a moment too long—not enough to send him crashing, but enough to allow him to recognize and correct his errors. He progressed down, frisking from side to side, growing in confidence and comfort through each fulcrum throughout his line. By the midpoint, he dipped in and out of each turn, riding a wave of his own design. He smiled as the mountain opened to his command and accelerated into the rush of air and cold sprinkles that kissed his lips. The rush filled his spirit to the bounds of the valley: from the soles of his feet, to the imprint in the slope where he fell, to the upper rim of the bowl, and to whatever lies beyond that. It was a silent exclamation, which Godric cared not to name but could be summarized in a single notion: *this is freedom.*

The leveled basin extinguished the thrust of gravity and smothered Godric's speed with hydraulic pressure from its snowy drifts. His skis foiled over the surface for a moment until they waned into the snow. The colors of his skis disappeared as his feet submerged into depths of white. The snow hugged his shins, embracing him to a sudden stop. Godric's chest lunged forward against the jolt of his own momentum. His hands tossed back over his shoulders, and his head lifted in a protective response. The response was instinctual, but he held the pose as if marking a crescendo. He was alone at the bottom of the basin, surrounded by a bleached canvas and encased by the glass of the sky. The gentle snowfall sang a romantic serenade around his orange coat as if Godric were the subject of a masterpiece.

The mountain voiced a pledge of tranquility with a hush that ran from the bowl's summit to its base. Resting at the base, Godric felt suspended in its province. Reeves glided past him in silence, tucking and rising in long parabolas that carried the teacher to the lift. Godric shook his head, laughing as he watched his coach float by, noting another lesson as he trekked in pursuit.

The chairlift settled after connecting to the high-speed line with its two riders resting in kind. Reeves clasped the open shoulder around the bench, outlining a plot for the coming runs. Godric's hands pressed into his lap as if holding the experience as a fragile heirloom.

The rotors of the passing lift pole sent a soft tremble through the chair, breaking the silence. The action captured Godric's attention, and he admired the machinery's work—the wheels rolled as they were designed in union with a thousand components constructed under a single intention to carry them up the mountain. He marveled at the confidence—the audacity—of the men who draft such machines and state with certainty that they will safely transport masses of people at lethal heights over the span of decades. Those men set a new purpose for the naked range long before the tall girders rose from the ground, freeing man to explore and frolic in the once inaccessible backcountry. *What ability!* Godric thought, to possess a faculty of sight that projects beyond what it observes; that sees beyond the potential of crude earth; that beholds its final form given shape by his own image. Man is cursed for his ego, but what other word is there for a man who glances at the beauty of nature and sees what glory sprouts from the seeds of his own ingenuity? A question occurred to Godric as he thought of the architects. He turned to Reeves.

"Why did you wait to tell me how to navigate powder until after I fell?" Godric said.

Reeves nodded, acknowledging the spirit of the question.

"Could you have waited? Would you have listened over the mountain's call?" Reeves responded.

"It would have been helpful to know before I dropped in."

"It's right to ask, but sometimes an answer to a question has no value. It can't become a lesson until there's something to learn. Knowledge is a funny thing. When you stand on top of a run like that, you see the white cover as solid, tangible matter. But you have to engage with it to understand. Yes, it's solid, but when you jump in, it acts like air. Then, it reacts like a fluid. It's all of those things all at once. I can tell you this now because you experienced it. You felt it. I give you the words for something you already understand. But you needed that base of experience to build on first. When you're standing at the top, I can give you knowledge. When you're dusting yourself off after a hard fall, the lesson serves your own wisdom."

"I get it," Godric said. His eyes narrowed and locked on Reeves as a recital of his words.

"Then tell me," Reeves said, handing the role of teacher back to his student.

"Tell you what?"

"What wisdom do you have now that you didn't when you dropped in?"

Godric's face took the shape of amused delight as a surge of nostalgia transported him back to his university seminars, where he participated in lectures as if he were playing a game. A spirited student with high regard for his studies can make learning a contest. Godric never shied away from a professor's challenge, even when—perhaps, especially when—he disagreed with them. The ruse Reeves employed was familiar, and Godric almost raised his hand to spring his teacher's trap.

"The mountain is a reflection," Godric answered. "It grants what a skier brings to it. A brash skier will sprawl in snow as deep as his own insolence. But focused aggression brings speed, and disciplined technique secures control. Then bring just enough of a daredevil attitude to enjoy it."

Godric paused and, with the cadence of a comedic punchline, added, "Of course, your question excludes the most important lesson I learned today."

"Which was?" Reeves asked, his own face mirroring Godric's amusement.

"If you're not close to falling, you're not getting better," Godric delivered with a smirk of Reeves' righteousness.

"Atta boy," Reeves said, avowing the lesson Godric imparted back at him.

The steel cable carried the chair across as a bridge to the far end of Offering Bowl and The Seraph's highest peak. For the first time in two weeks, a crack broke the rocky shell of gray clouds, and the sapphire sky gleamed like a precious gem within the rift. The crack widened. Men instinctively rise in the presence of the noble, the honorable, the virtuous. The sight of blue sky piercing the clouds summoned that same reflex in Reeves. He lifted his skis until the tips scored the hem of the floating jewel. Reeves held the sky as the setting for a treasure or grand reward. As he witnessed its beauty, a quiet satisfaction settled over him, and he gave praise for the world, his student, himself, and the existence of his chosen profession.

In the hours that followed, Reeves and Godric exhausted the back side bowls of The Fourth

Seraph, section-by-section, following an orbital path along the rim and choosing runs like the hour hand of a clock. With each tick, Reeves reiterated his instructions, adding nuance to his lessons. Godric absorbed the guidance, adjusting his form with each insight Reeves shared. With each improvement, Reeves commanded a dozen more refinements for Godric's technique. Reeves' advice seemed as endless as the mountain itself, and, in an unconscious admission, Godric understood the value Reeves sought in pursuit of the ever-improving and a seemingly unreachable perfection.

Through each run, Godric's comfort and skill progressed to the point where he felt poised to make more daring experiments. He charged down for speed until he felt the tug of an undertow pull beneath him. He held the fall line up to the moment his path would collapse, only to pull up with all his might. The snow swelled against his skis and peeled beneath them. The swirling current carried him up, and Godric rode the white tide toward the sky. The cap of his helmet emerged from the frozen smoke fouetting around him and continued until Godric's heels reached the crest of the braking surface.

There was no thrust behind him nor stroke of feathers that sent him into the air. Godric claimed neither ground nor air but simply found himself suspended, yet still animated, at the center of his own universe. There, the mountain held him in tribute upon a flying pedestal and left him feeling that, if he held on long enough, it would carry him beyond the heavens. At that moment, his sense of joy became more vivid than sight, and his capacity for happiness seemed as limitless as the infinite sky above him and the bottomless snow below.

Their trek brought vast fields, narrow glades littered with trees, sudden drops, and buried boulders dressed as ramps under the thick snow. Every leg of the expedition brought a new challenge, and with each run, Godric added a new addendum to his own definition of freedom. It was only the spiring shadows inching over the slopes that reminded Godric of his perilous delimiter: time.

It was midafternoon when their trip reached the last section of the bowl. They stood at the rim's edge, not far from where Godric crashed. Godric searched for the markings, but the winter snowfall erased the scene left by his fall. He turned to the slope below him. He let the sunlight pour over him from the opening in the sky and lifted his goggles to the bright glare over the wintery landscape. Brilliant light brings an ache to dim eyes. Godric winced as his sight adjusted but forced his eyes to a wide aperture, wishing to remember everything: the image of the mountain vista imprinted with all the emotions the day granted. With two heavy breaths, the memory became permanent, and Godric reset his goggles, closing the shutter.

Even the vigor of youth cannot escape the eventuality of fatigue; the day's toil ruptured in Godric's legs at the bottom of the run. The deepest fibers in his thighs swelled in full flex even as he stood relaxed in line. They quivered as he stretched, and he massaged the tight flesh with his palms, squeezing with a wish to purge all pain, fear, and the lingering flaw in his genetics from his body. He knew the shaking was from overuse, the throbbing aftershocks from the long day. He told himself that it was a potent mixture of rigor and adrenaline and pushed away any thoughts of his condition, thinking, *it no longer matters.*

"I think I'm done," Godric said, bent over with his fingers still kneading his legs."

Reeves' hand dubbed his student's shoulder in consolation, in solemnity, and in blessing.

"It's a good day," Reeves said and held his hand on Godric's shoulder for a moment. He added two firm pats and then waived him forward toward the loading zone. "Let's go. We still have to make our way back to the base."

The sun settled in its lower meridian, marking the hour of alpine twilight for skiers across The Seraphs. Skiing is a pilgrimage for those who do not live in the mountains. Every run is a spiritual act, a devotion unto itself. And day and night are not separated by light and dark but by celebration and tranquility. Reeves and Godric sat, sated, as their cable car ferried them from the depths of Offering Bowl back to the face of The Seraphs.

"It was a good day," Godric affirmed as he collapsed against the chair back. The long moments of pause failed to interrupt their conversation.

"Time spent on the mountain is never a waste," Reeves said.

"A proverb! The guy from your article finally comes out."

"He's always here, just below the surface. The words of my conscience. Sometimes, they escape my mouth."

"I think I have been hearing them all day, *Brother*."

"Now, don't let's start with that," Reeves said with a laugh that shook the bench.

"But you have been preaching all day. And I followed as your disciple."

"Fair, but I never asked for that. Just like I never asked for that nickname."

"I know you didn't ask for it. You demanded it. You set the terms on our first ride up. You used a word for what you train your students to be."

"Aesthete," Reeves said in answer to the unasked.

"And I got a taste of that. Now, I'm hooked. I'm in your cult. I won't ever be what you are, but I'm certain I'll spend the rest of my life trying."

"Then you are."

"How?"

"My aim and what I teach is not an achievement or a title. It's not something that is bestowed upon you. It's for the taking. It's a pursuit. It's a state, a noun that's a verb. It's like being alive. You are until you're not."

"Until we're not," Godric said, proposing a toast to his teacher and the day that had passed. Godric raised his pole, and Reeves returned in kind. Metal kissed metal in salute to kindred souls.

The journey out of the back bowls carried riders over the plateau of The Fourth Seraph. Broken rock and steep cliffs marred the long ridge, making it inaccessible for skiers and incompatible with the sport. Deep pools of snow collected sparse divots spread across the terrain, leaving white craters in the bare rock face that otherwise refused to hold the snowfall. The plateau served as a barrier that split the world in two: the carefully curated runs of the front side and the wild frontier of the back bowls. The vertex could not reconcile the two. Once passed, a skier had no vision of the other side. All that was before them was a final judgment and immediate sentence. The mountain's trail map gave no name to the summit, but locals dubbed it Arch Angel.

Myths speak truth even if fabricated in the lore of history. The testament of Offering Bowl's own history told such a truth. Its legends whispered of a great battle over the valley long before Western settlers occupied the land. Overwhelmed and facing defeat, the defending natives placed a curse over the land before their final retreat so that any man who entered the surrendered valley would never be allowed to leave. Reeves and Godric escaped the valley as their chairlift crossed over Arch Angel, but it could be said that they, too, fell to the curse. They departed in body but left their souls entangled with their experience. The valley vanished behind the eastward ridge but would be carried in whole by their spirit, however long their days.

A light flurry descended from the broken clouds

hovering over The Seraphs as the sun shined in the open crease between the horizon and the passing front. Over a fortnight, skiers basked in the violent, furious blessings that swept over the deep range until this, the last breath of a relentless arctic storm.

Frail flakes, devoid of their strength, dissolved as they landed on the orange and blue shells of the two men standing on the flat highlands of The Fourth Seraph. The pair said nothing. In the silence, Godric thought to himself, they shouldn't call this a resort; it's an enclave that grants freedom in its confines. Life imitates art, and the summit of The Fourth Seraph reduced all existence to its grand amphitheater. The hardened wall behind Godric and Reeves provided the backdrop, and beyond its proscenium waited an audience of sharp jags that stretched off in layered rows of rocky peaks across the deep range. Within the stage of a theater, there lies an entire universe, scripted with infinite possibilities limited only by its own dimensions and the imagination of a playwright. In a play, the stage is filled with choices, and the mountain presented infinite paths to the two skiers; still, they all pointed in a single direction: down.

"Which way?" Godric asked, citing a new line in their living script.

"There. North Star." Reeves said, pointing as he read the trail sign that marked a path partway down the hill. "We will use the old ways. Our ancestors followed the North Star, and so will we. It's the first leg of Constellation, the longest route on the mountain. It starts here and runs to the base of The Second Seraph: North Star to Orion's Belt; Orion's Belt to Dipper; Dipper to Milky Way; and Milky Way, home."

Conversation is as brittle as time; one phrase passes to make room for the next. But like moments in history, some words come to stand as instant monuments in the depths of our psyche. *Home* was such a word for Godric. The idea twisted Godric's mind like an unanswerable riddle. A home is raised and measured over shared lifetimes. It is a strange inheritance whose equity is spiritual and dissolves upon a man's maturity—to be rebuilt of his own accord. *Home* dissolved for Godric in the days after his diagnosis, and it remained an incompatible concept for a man whose view only extended as far as the day's horizon. Even so, he found the idea worthy of worship, so as Reeves spoke, *home* landed on a waiting pedestal in Godric's mind.

The sacred provokes an acute psychological response that commands a man to grovel in humility or rise in glory. Godric sought beauty and immersed himself in the panoramic splendor saturating the promontory, even if for the last time. Beauty is a powerful stimulant for the soul. Godric felt his spirit stretch, weaving into the sight the stitch of his own absolute judgment that said, as a matter of fact: *this is good*. He turned to the valley and saw the slanted rooftops bowing in homage. In that moment, he felt that they did not bend to the majesty of the mountain but to the men who stood atop its ground and dared to make such judgments. Godric thought, let the measure of my lifetime not be in years but by moments like this.

"I feel more at home right now on this peak than anywhere I've lived for a long while," Godric said, responding to the moment as much to his partner's words.

"That's good," Reeves said, nodding.

"Why do you say that?"

"You're like me. This isn't a hobby or a sport. It's a love. And the difference between a house and a home is that a home is packed with the things that you love—a spouse; children; artwork; food; our ski gear; giant theater systems to transform watching TV series, films, and sporting events into a living experience. You fill a home with your love so that it reflects and fills you with that same love. That's what you're feeling right now."

"How do you know it?"

"Because I feel it too."

With that, Reeves laid down his duty as teacher. The lesson was over. The parting wisdom drew a final truth, which they both understood, and as teacher, Reeves had the honor of stating aloud. It exposed the root of what gravitated Godric to Reeves when they met at the Steep Easy. Members of shared species flock and grow as an evolutionary imperative. Men flock as a spiritual imperative. Godric volunteered, and Reeves adopted him into his own dynasty. In the dynamics of age, one cannot discern who learns more in the relationship between master and protégé, student and teacher, and parent and child. What was passed between them was just as foundational and transcendent as the values and heredity that span the generations of a family.

Without any further instructions, the pair set off towards North Star. Reeves dropped in first, taking the front but not the lead. Instead, he served only as guide through the interconnected trails of Constellation and left Godric to end his run in any way he saw fit.

Reeves dashed into his line with his spectrum of

skill on full display. Long arcs gave him speed. His velocity carried him into tight, twisting turns that, at first glance, should have left the mountain raveled in knots, yet the slope seemed to be unwinding beneath his feet. The patterns varied; Reeves picked the moves that moved him. The coordination of his joints spoke with exquisite articulation—his ankles, knees, the space between every vertebrae, his shoulders, and arms all moved in unison. His body cranked like a piston through the turns, and Reeves owned the attention of every skier he passed. Those on the slope saw him flying by in a time-lapse, and those above saw him caught in slow motion. Both groups captured but snapshots—single frames of a motion that showed a man with an intransigent posture: upright, unbroken, and unbreakable. No music followed him, but the distinct impression of a musical score accompanied Reeves as he passed through the sight of his audience. His timing was rhythmic and movement, melodic with all the depth and spectacle of a full orchestra. Reeves skied in a song that hypnotized onlookers and transcended his mechanical precision into elegance and grace.

Reeves skied a symphony, Godric a quartet.

Reeves provided no guidance for their final run, and Godric did not recall any specific instructions.

Instead, he held the composite form of the day's every lesson as an integrated sum: learning, adapting, and predicting, all in reflection of Reeve's training. Two skis fixed to bound legs as an indivisible sum that followed the cues from outstretched hands. Godric's wrists snapped ahead of each turn, setting off a cascade of motion. The lessons gave him an outlet for his own expression. Any musical composition is subject to interpretation by a conductor. Godric played his own variations on Reeves' theme. He set his own cadence and, like his teacher, chose a line and movements for the sole purpose of his own delight.

And Godric found joy to be a powerful anesthetic. The strands of muscles burned in his legs as they pulled him in and out of every turn, but the pain was overwhelmed by the ecstasy brought by the action. Each turn led into the next, and Godric's conscious condensed his entire existence into the line he skied. There, pain was of no consequence. There, his fate was of no consequence. There, was a world devoid of malady.

Reeves guided their path to the waypoints between Orion's Belt and Dipper. Godric followed, skiing with his own autonomy. Still, it was clear that, as the pair navigated the paths of Constellation, they both offered their own devotion to a shared mission. A strange thread of time seemed to tie them together. The thread braided present and prophecy. At once, Godric skied behind Reeves as his shadow —an approximate shape that mimicked the movement of his master—yet he was a mold of his teacher's raw material, still unfinished, that seemed to cast a projection of its final shape in the man who skied before him.

Many people saw the performance, but few understood. The sun flashed on Dipper like a spotlight, shining over a populous of skiers finishing their day. Their day skiing in solitude ended. Reeves and Godric maneuvered through the mass of locals, tourists, and mountain staff with indifference as if they were no more than the trees and boulders they evaded all afternoon. They bounded in endless transitions between heavy mass and weightlessness, splashing the shimmering glitter of sunkissed snow into the air as they passed. Through their final run, eyes turned toward them in unison as if pulled by a wand that tilted the heads of each person they passed. Most dismissed what they saw; no more than every tenth person stopped to admire. Awe calls to men in a language that few understand. Those who understood held the vision long into their memory in an enduring admiration for the men dancing down the slopes and commanding the mountain as a tamed beast. Their recognition carried a silent applause in gratitude and in inspiration to be carried in all their days to follow. The rest remained oblivious to the two men living the best day of their lives.

The valley's edge cast a curtained shadow over Milkyway as Godric and Reeves approached the base. The topcoat of snow remained loose, and the base, strong, even after a full day of traffic. The gradual slope was a gentle smile even for the most novice skiers on the mountain. Their final run was the easiest of the day, and the two cruised to the end of the terrain, cutting through the lattice of tracks and adding their own trails to the exhibits left by tired skiers.

The hours of high ascents and floating upon wing-tipped skis expired; the two aesthetes returned to the mountain floor. The flat earth at the base felt like an alien world, and walking seemed like an unnatural movement. Godric jettisoned his skis and hiked toward Reeves using his poles and skis to stabilize his steps. Reeves remained mounted in his equipment and leaned out over his poles, which braced his shoulders as girders as he looked up toward the mountain.

"The lifts will still be open for a bit longer. There's still time to get in another lap or two," Reeves said with his head resting on his shoulder and leaning into the proverbial devil upon it.

"I'd rather stop one run too soon than one run too late," Godric said, hiding one truth behind another.

"Today was a good day. Thank you for booking me."

"Was it the best day of your life?"

"You already know the answer to that. How about you?"

"With absolute honesty, I can tell you that if I leave this world today, it would not have been a waste. Please remember that."

Reeves removed his glove and extended his hand. Godric followed his teacher's lead for the last time. A weak gust breezed across their exposed flesh. Their palms, moist with warm sweat, breathed a steaming fog that dissolved into the winter. The sharp cold did not bite but felt refreshing against all exhaustion. Their hands embraced, and each felt the comfort of the other's warmth blanket around his hand.

"When you come back, be sure to book me again," Reeves said.

"You're certain I will come back?" Godric said.

"You're not done skiing this mountain. Not after a day like this. I am as certain of that as I am that I will be back out here tomorrow."

"That's a safe bet. But I thought I couldn't afford you."

"We'll make it work."

"Thanks, *Brother*."

"It was my pleasure."

Their arms dropped, neither noticing that their hands clasped far longer than custom and through all of their parting words. Godric took leave and trekked off toward the far end of the base lodge. With fixed eyes staring straight ahead, he never looked back. Godric hiked away in a straight line as if following a map. Reeves unsnapped his bindings and started marching toward the staff locker room. He turned back and watched Godric's orange coat grow smaller in the distance until it disappeared into the crowd.

"So long, you old son of a bitch," Godric whispered aloud to the cold, winter air.

Reeves found a nearby rack and brushed the snow off his skis. A painter must clean his brushes and pallet at the end of a session. So it was with Reeves. With meticulous care, he scraped the packed snow stuck within the crevasses of his bindings and ran his hands up and down the planes of each ski. Once they were as clean as when he started, he unzipped his coat, pulled out his phone, and dialed the number for the ski school booking agency.

"Hello, Holly," Reeves greeted the agent across the line.

"How did it go today?" Holly asked.

"He was a no-show. " Reeves said.

"Should I charge him the normal fees?" Holly's voice asked with a hint of confusion.

"No, waive the fees. No need to punish him. He's young and probably bailed out when he realized how expensive I am."

"Okay. I will take care of it."

"Thank you, Holly. Anything for tomorrow?"

"No," Holly said, "you're free tomorrow."

"Thank you."

"Oh, and Zack, one more thing before you go," Holly added.

"Yes?"

"That kid—the no-show—he just called here to add a hundred-dollar tip. Care to explain?"

"Waive the fees, and have a good night, Holly," Reeves ended the call, smiling.

Part Five: *The Falls*

If God separated the day and night, The Seraphs brought them back together. The storm front left the deep range, and a slim crescent moon christened the delicate blue sky amid the lingering daylight. Climbing shadows lifted The Seraph's bright snowcaps upon its pedestal, and the distant cloud bank highlighted the mountain's luster as it cradled the white slopes as a precious pearl. Reeves remained by his skis, finding it as difficult to let go of the day as the daylight defying the night.

Reeves lifted his skis from the rack and took two steps before stopping to let the tails of the long planks rest on the ground. The brief reflection became a manifold of emotion. A tingling, radiating warmth swelled beneath his eyes. The day pried open whatever shell encased his soul. He shared his world and his love more completely with Godric than any student he ever taught. And he saw the birth of that world re-manifest within his pupil. Reeves had no articulate for what he felt. Gratitude and satisfaction were concepts too small … for a world that offered this work … that Reeves could choose it … and that together, they would yield a day such as this. The emotion was as absolute as the mountain was immovable. Reeves turned back toward the slope to acknowledge both. His sight was a salute and valediction to the day that was and all the days to come.

This is my backyard; Reeves thought as his eyes traced the four peaks of The Seraphs. Reeves spread his conscious over the whole of the mountain to mark his own sovereign kingdom. His eyes cast a blessing, and the image reflected it back toward him. Gratitude dripped with disbelief in the thoughts that followed: *That I get to spend my days like this. That exhilaration and ecstasy is the common, and passion, the standard without exception. That no matter how many times it's repeated, my life on The Seraphs never becomes routine.*

The more skiers fled the slopes, the more he felt the slopes his property. He smiled at the last few skiers riding the chairlifts, squeezing every last run and every bit of joy they could from the mountain. He felt no resentment toward them, happy to share his backyard with any man who sought what he sought. There were not many left; the lifts carried only a handful of skiers. Reeves watched long strings of empty chairs climb toward the sky. Soon, they would stop, and the quiet darkness would follow to set the stage for Reeves to do it all again in the morning.

An aberration flashed inside an all-too-familiar sight and disrupted Reeves' farewell.

Was that?…No, he thought, it couldn't be. Fleeting visions leave more doubt than certainty, so Reeves re-traced his glance across the mountain. At first, he saw nothing unusual throughout the shaded runs and trees, only sparse skiers at the end of their day. Then, his eyes followed a lift reeling up The Second Seraph. On it, he saw a lone rider cross the threshold of the valley's shadow, and, emerging in the sunlight, he saw the unmistakable spark of bright fluorescent orange.

Answer preceded inquiry as Reeves cross-examined thoughts before they fully formed in his mind. He recalled every question Godric asked about *The Falls*. They were too curious and too smart, and Reeves' own answers gave away too much. They led Godric to that lift, where it dropped its riders, and a skier who possesses such answers knows the deathly line from there. He remembered Godric's parting words in the shape of that map. Reeves realized what he drew for Godric: Salt Mine Express down a mix of trails to Two-and-a-Half Pass, through Hallow's Gallows; and finally a chute down *The Falls*. With the map clear in his mind, he heard Godric's voice speaking over it; *if I leave this world today, it would not have been a waste. Please remember that.*

The heels of Reeves' ski boots left a chain of divots in the ground behind him. He added new links with each bounding step as he ran awkwardly toward the lift, where he saw the orange spark. As he ran, his attention followed Godric's chair as it climbed. At the crest of a ridge, he saw a flare of sunlight reflect against the lens of Godric's goggles. Godric was looking back at him as the chair disappeared behind the ridgeline. Reeves' vision could no longer account for his student, and his apprehension fell to dread. He cursed the clumsy mechanics of his boots and the heavy equipment in his arms as he tried to run faster. When he reached the tail of the lift line, he tossed his skis to the ground, planted both poles, and mounted his boots in tandem, with the flair of a gymnast.

"Squeezing in one last run?" the lift operator asked Reeves as he waited for a chair.

"One last run," Reeves said, short of breath.

A chair swept under his kneecaps, and Reeves' spine pressed against the slats behind him. He felt the chair accelerate as it began its ascent, and all he could think of was Godric unloading at the top.

The first lift tower he passed held a sign that read, "Check for Loose Clothing/Equipment." Reeves was disheveled, as restless in body as in thought. He frantically checked all his equipment. His goggles hung off the back of his unstrapped helmet. The zipper of his jacket was still half-open, and the straps of his gloves clung to the wrists of his uncovered hands. Reeves explored his gear but could not bring himself to marshall any order. He felt paralyzed by the anxiety that he had no real action to take except to wait out his ride.

The memory of a protocol clicked in his helplessness. Reeves slapped the chest pockets in his glacier blue coat. He felt his cell phone against one breast, and on the other, he found an object with a rounded base and protruding point. His palm clasped the outer shell of his jacket around the hand-held radio. It was his only alternative to waiting. A moment later, the device sat in his palm. A small green light glowed at the edge of the radio's dark gray plastic, and its antenna was still tuned to the mountain's emergency channel.

His thumb hovered over the intercom. He moved to press it, but his body refused. Reeves shook his head as if the physical act could dissolve the picture of Godric looking back at him on the chairlift. He tried again; this time, his thumb responded and compressed the button, only to release it a moment later. Reeves was unable to speak.

Why does this matter to me so much? Reeves asked himself as he froze, not from the cold but from a foreboding warning in his conscience. He thought of the thousands of lessons over his career; none were like today's. Reeves' thoughts continued: through all those lessons, I taught my technique and style, but Godric opened himself to my teaching in a way no other student had. Godric listened without barrier or filter and let my teachings reach the roots of his mind. It was an act so honest as to invoke my own unfiltered honesty.

It is a paradox that a truth in nature is immutable, but honesty in a man is a vulnerability. An idea shared in honesty is a sharp blade. If handed to an honest companion, the idea will return tempered, polished, and honed. If handed to a dishonest opponent, he will wield it as a weapon. What courage it takes to stand and speak without the shelter of decorum or conformity—to speak as Godric did at the Steep Easy. These thoughts passed through Reeves' mind with a revelation: honesty is intellectual intimacy.

Reeves' eyes glazed in the harrowing dizziness of

the chairlift's height, and his deep deliberation sent him further into a trance of thought. I've only just met this kid, and I'll likely never see him again, he thought. Is it irrational to harbor such strong feelings? The idea of romantic love at first sight is laughable. Still, it is common within familial love. Parents and siblings bestow an infant child with immediate and infinite love. But Godric is a grown man, and a grown man must earn such a gift from another. What has he earned from me?

Everything, Reeves thought. My reward as a teacher is the teaching. Being on the snow and sharing what I have learned and developed was all I thought I wanted, but this kid gave me something new. It was not just that he accepted my lessons so willingly or reflected what he learned. It's that what I saw was not a reflection at all. I saw Godric's own image showing me the deep qualities that I strive to cultivate in myself. Together, we lived a day, broke bread, and explored the mountain on skis. And all the while, we discovered the entire meaning of life: filling our capacity for joy, engaging nature, demonstrating the beauty of the human body, and stimulating deep contemplation. I wish that could be taught, but it cannot be learned, at least not in a ski lesson. It either exists in a man or does not. It exists in me as it does in Godric. Why is that so rare?

In teaching, I impart lessons, but today, it was more, as if I passed on a part of myself to Godric. And that created a fraternal bond. Men who share parents are but brothers. Men who share values are brethren. That's what Godric is. Even if I never see him again, I could live out my days in satisfaction, knowing that he exists. If he dies, then that part of me dies as well, as well as that rare trait in him that I, too, share. I never wanted a legacy, but now that I know one of this kind can exist, I want it to live on in him. How strange it is that conviction within one man's life can be impervious yet so fragile between generations.

The base of the radio slipped to Reeves's lap as his hand went limp. Reeves knew ski patrol could reach Godric first. Patrollers would be corralling people off the backside and shutting down the top lifts soon. Reeves thought that if he didn't call ski patrol, Godric's body would be found and identified, and investigators would question the ski instructor he hired. They'd check his ski pass to find which line Godric climbed The Second Seraph. They would also find that Reeves followed shortly after. He would be fired, if not worse. If he radioed ski patrol, a team would scramble and be waiting for Godric at the edge of Hallows Gallows. Reeves imagined the border of the tree line and thought of the group of skiers he stopped yesterday. He replayed the scene in front of Hallow's Gallows but instead saw—with clarity—the patrollers escorting Godric off the mountain and banning him from The Seraphs. He watched Godric's face scowl, knowing who betrayed him. Whatever reason Godric chose to end his life by skiing *The Falls*, a ski patroller sending him away would make it all the worse. If it's not *The Falls* today, it will be something else, eventually.

"That's not what he needs," Reeves said aloud to his own conscience.

Reeves tucked the radio back into his pocket.

The ride up Divine Eagle reached its final leg, marked by a sign that read, "Prepare to unload." The act of skiing is marred by frustrating stretches of waiting. A skier starts his day in wait: forty-five minutes standing in lift lines and sitting through multiple lifts before reaching his first skiable run. Meanwhile, the mountain tempts every helpless skier —captive within the walls of a gondola or in a cage of sheer height—with the vision of its vast landscapes and seductive, yet unreachable, slopes. Homer wrote of Odysseus warning his crew of the sea-faring sirens on his journey to Ithaca, but

Homer left no warning for Reeves. Godric's fate made the waiting worse. But his choice was made, and, just as the pace of the wind limited Odysseus's crew, he continued his journey at the pace of the mountain.

Reeves left the off-ramp on Divine Eagle, skirting toward the base of Salt Mine Express.

"The lift is closed, *preacher-man*," the lift operator said, recognizing Reeves' blue coat, confusing his nickname, this time as an intentional joke. "It's time to head back down for beers and whiskey," he added with a playful, carefree smile.

Chairs continued to swing through the loading zone. Reeves knew that meant the lift's last riders were still being carried up. Closed gates blocked the loading zone. Reeves ignored the warning and tried to slip past the posts. The lift operator stepped in front of him.

"Hold up right there," the operator said, placing his hands on Reeves's shoulders but holding his smile, hoping to de-escalate the situation. "I already called the last rider to the boys upstairs. We're fixing to shut down as soon as he unloads."

"Was he wearing an orange coat?" Reeves asked.

"What?"

"Dammit! The last rider, what color was his

coat?" Reeves insisted, his voice more stern than loud.

"Yeah, yeah, it was bright orange like a hunter. Couldn't miss it. He loaded a little while ago. He's probably up near the top by now."

"Listen, I don't care what you tell the team up at the terminal. Give whatever excuse you want, blame me, or say whatever you need to cover your ass. I am getting on this lift."

The operator pulled his hands off Reeves' shoulder. He kept his hands raised, forgetting to drop them when he saw the grave look upon Reeves' brow. The lift operator's playful smile dissolved and matched Reeves' tone. The operator understood the seriousness of the situation.

"Last rider just jettisoned down Dark Adits. Confirm shutdown. Over," the radio called from inside the operator's hut.

The lift operator watched Reeves' body shudder at the announcement and the cost of each passing chair. Reeves's anxiety grew and passed to the lift operator. The deep sobriety told the operator that, whatever the matter, Reeves had to attend to the matter himself and he should ask for no further details. The lift operator shook his head and then nodded in succession. Reeves knew he understood.

"Okay. What can I do? Can I call for patrollers? Medics? Anything?"

"Just get me up there."

The operator reached into the lift hut, opened the gates, and pulled out a radio handset.

"Sorry, fellas," he spoke into the radio. "I'm calling in a favor and loading one more rider. He's on his way up on chair ninety-three. I got soft and couldn't say no to a staffer begging for one more run in these epic conditions. And before you say anything, first round is on me tonight."

"Thank you," Reeves said.

"Good luck, *brother.*"

The lift operator placed the corded radio back on its bracket in the lift hut, waved Reeves through the open gates, and then signaled him to wait. Two chairs passed before number ninety-three swung around the bullwheel. The operator grabbed his broom, swept the loose snow off its bench, and pointed, saying, "Here's your ride." Reeves caught the chair, and the operator watched him carefully until he disappeared from sight.

Reeves bare hand stopped as he reached for the safety bar. He abandoned his own security and began preparation, knowing that the run to come called for every ounce of aggression he could muster. His helmet clasped under his jaw, and its strap brushed between his chin and the zipped-up collar on his jacket. His gloves pulled tight over his hands and stretched them over his sleeves, squeezing off every ounce of drag he could. Reeves calculated that Godric's head start was at least fifteen minutes, and, even with his skill, he was not sure he could make up that much time. The edge of the bench became his starting line. Reeves crept forward until he felt the crossbar press under the balls of his hips. He took every bit that gravity afforded. The gain of an extra inch was more important than the long fall to the ground.

Hanging on the edge of the chair, Reeves pressed his thumbs through the length of his thighs. Every muscle activated in a chain of contractions that ran through his body. He squeezed his toes and flexed his calves. Twitching legs sent a warm shiver through his outstretched spine and rolling shoulders. He felt the weight of his blood dangling in his feet as he held his balance on the chair's edge. Reeves then took a series of deep breaths and hard exhales until a warm radiance permeated his flesh and could be seen in the stacks of condensed air leaving his mouth.

When the terminal of Salt Mine Express came

into view, Reeves closed his eyes and saw the entirety of the mountain in his blindness. The mountain converged as his mind expanded. Dark Adits…Mine Bender…Railcart catwalk…Denominator…Two-and-a-Half Pass—the full chain of runs that led him to Hallows Gallows blended into a condensed synopsis in his conscious. Reeves' thoughts divided and accelerated to the point where he visualized and processed every turn along the path all at once. His anticipation was so thorough that it left no room for surprises and no need for reaction. He needed only to act. He opened his eyes as the chair rolled over the last tower, and, as a mantra, as a prayer, as a commandment to his body, he said: "Let's go."

The hinge of chair ninety-three sent a strident screech over the peak of The Second Seraph as it recoiled. Reeves' hips snapped forward, and his arms sent a thrust of power that launched him down the off-ramp. Reeves dashed toward Dark Adits and disappeared with such speed that the lift operators thought the screaming sound of the lift was that of a rider falling off a chair. Before the lift crew could engage the lift's emergency stop, Reeves was long gone in his pursuit of Godric.

Reeves preserved the economy of distance, making minimal turns, just enough to keep him in optimal position as he entered Mine Bender. Speed came from an effortless acceleration. Reeves skied with racer's offensive, but his body kept his signature tight form, cutting through the air with the ease of a whetted blade. The mountain seemed to grant him a pardon from the laws of physics, awarding more speed while excusing him from the limits of terminal velocity.

A line of skiers and coaches waited at the starting gates at the top of Mine Bender. The national team made its final training runs, making up for time lost during the midday blizzard. A coach called out the racers' time to the first gates—it was the fastest start of the day. The group watched the race clock with rapt attention as the racer tracked a course record. They did not see Reeves approaching.

The slope dropped beneath Reeves's skis as he passed the ridgeline between Dark Adits and Mine Bender. As the mountain face fell, Reeves soared. He tucked his knees into his chest and found more speed as he flew through the air. When he approached the Earth, he leaned sideways and pressed his legs outward, beginning a turn in mid-air. He landed on the edge of his skis, and his shoulders swept a coat of blue-dyed snow off the middle of the racecourse. The closing of the turn sent him upright, and he zoomed toward the racer in mid-run. The racer wore a red, skin-tight unitard garnished with a green bib that flapped in the wind. The racer streaked down the course but could not escape Reeves. The gap between them closed. Coaches and other competitors cursed—first in astonishment, then in fear—as they watched Reeves close in from their perch above the staring gates. Their loud hollers echoed above the triumphal archway as they witnessed the two skiers on a collision course. The calls were futile; both skiers out-raced the sound.

Reeves saw the green-bibbed skier but kept his line, staying in chase but thinking only of the distance between himself and Godric. The gap between Reeves and the racer collapsed. Reeves swung outwards in a brief move to set up a hard turn. The group at the start gasped as if the move were a wind-up for Reeves to strike their best racer with a fatal blow. The racer continued his run, oblivious to the danger behind him. As Reeves' ski tips pulled even to the racer's heels, he cut right, sending a slash through the racer's trail and releasing a collective exhale from watchers atop the racecourse. Reeves' speed blurred his identity, and the group's anger turned to wonder over how a man could ski so fast.

The long skis bent into a semi-circle as Reeves made the hairpin turn up Railcart catwalk beyond a racer's speed. The skis flung him toward the catwalk in a sling-shot maneuver. Reeves held the turn as long as he could and pierced the center of the narrow path's entrance with precision, but he carried the lethal speed into the arching trail. He surged toward the catwalk's ledge and its steep drop into a thicket of dense trees. A crash would tear life from flesh. Reeves braced his legs: fighting against his own force, fighting for his life, fighting for Godric's. His speed was too much. The tips of his ski stretched beyond the cliff. Then the mid-ski followed. Just before his feet reached the edge, Reeves flexed his hips and flung his elbow upslope. He spun around as his feet breached the threshold, struggling to keep the fleeting pressure on the edge of his skis. He threw his body forward from the anchor of his boots, keeping his center of gravity over the catwalk while his feet hung over the cliff. His heels slanted upward as his skis flexed against the pressure. The further he slipped past the cliff, the more he lifted, until he stood on tiptoe with only the top ends of his skis left scraping the snow. He held the position with all the power and skill of a ballerina making a fouetté on pointe. With only a few inches of Earth left holding his life, the winding path twisted in Reeves' favor and brought him back over solid ground.

A buckshot of snow and ice pelted the forest from the barrels of Reeves' skis when they splashed down. A fine powder lingered in the air, following Reeves as he shot up the catwalk. The life-threatening force that pulled him toward the forest graveyard was now his ally, and it thrust him up the trail. Desperation turned to aggression. Hold your speed, Reeves thought and tucked his posture. He sat into his boots and brought his hands to a point to reduce his drag. Railcart's uphill climb forced even the fastest skiers into the slow crawl of cross-country course, but Reeves fired through the remainder of the empty catwalk.

Adrenaline coursed like a burning fuel through Reeves' veins. The faster his heart pumped, the slower his perception of time. When Railcart opened to the steep fall of Twining Denominator, the flow of Reeves' mind dilated. Where life allowed one thought per moment, Reeves could now take four. He moved with an acute awareness of his surroundings but a naive, almost innocent oblivion to his actions. He led the mountain in a dance down his favorite run. Each touch of his pole seemed to move the whole of the mountain, and the twisting path unwound into a straight line. For a moment, Reeves felt his consciousness saturate his surroundings and thought that he needn't turn at all. He needed but to hold straight, and the entirety of the globe would cater to his command, surrendering its axis to his feet and twisting along the tether of his will. If he but tugged its string, Reeves felt the Earth would bow before him as his loyal subject.

A true passion reduces a man's existence to a singularity that dissolves both choice and action—decisions vanish in a passionate man's resolve and action in his own certainty. It was once said that Reeves skied as a symphony, but he now skied as both performer and conductor: within the moment of the song and in full awareness of the melodies yet to come.

The heightened perception fused revelation and memory. Reeves recited Twining Denominator as a long scroll practiced a thousand times over. When he skied alone, he sought its slender confines and pinching curves because they left no room for error and demanded his best. Now, he found himself skiing inside a vivid premonition—powering through every turn yet to come and flying through the clearing at the run's end. He skied with abandon and without fear, taking for granted that his vision was inevitable.

The mountain submitted as Reeves seized absolute authority over his favorite run. He entered a long, narrow stretch as a procession, and Reeves' signature posture brought him to an upright, stalwart attention through the straightaway. Tree branches rustled in the wind, bending as nature's salute and honoring him as he passed. Through the remaining curves, Reeves skied in contradiction, hoarding power in the contours only to lay down his turns with a gentle caress. He ceded nothing to the mountain and kept all power for himself. The mountain became a tool for his disposal, no different than his skis and poles. He swept up the sides of the banked curves along the tight corners. He compressed under the pressure of his own force, pushing him into the hard banks. At the peak of each curve, he recoiled, plunging down the bank and returning any lost speed with interest.

And speed was all that mattered. Hot embers dwindle as they fall to the ground, but Reeves exercised a secret to keep the flame of his skiing bright. The hotter he burned, the more control he wielded. He never skied as such; in all his years, he never needed to. It was only now, with Godric's life at stake, that Reeves raised his ability to a new height. Reeves valued his student such that the scale of his own life tipped with Godric's fate in the balance. Reeves mined the entirety of his skill and experience to stretch his skiing from the pinnacle of mastery into omnipotence. He needed it. Only a god would dare ski through the thick bush of Hallow's Gallows.

Reeves found the blemish in Two-and-a-half Pass's rim when he reached the clearing. The day's storm left mounds of untouched snow on the outer banks of the open crater. Reeves' course sent him straight toward a gash in the brim and the footprints that led to it. The broken edge showed where Godric entered Hallow's Gallow. Reeves made haste, flying straight toward the opening Godric left.

Reeves traced Godric's footprints until they disappeared at the fringe of the forest. The dense foliage behind the rim's upper lip pulled a canopy over sight. Vision is man's first guard against fear— darkness and uncharted territory strip man of this basic defense. Hallow's Gallows had both. Light diffused behind the front line of trees, making the forest look both impenetrable and impassable. Timid thoughts burn in the incinerator of purpose. Every rule set to preserve safety and warn of danger vaporized in Reeves' conviction against certain death. The vacuum of shadows consumed his bright blue coat as Reeves ramped over the rim where Godric entered the forest.

A silent grunt flared from Reeves' nostrils as he clenched his jaw, flying over the crater's upper lip. His momentum pulled him airborne, but Reeves inverted the jump, imploding his knees at the peak to absorb the shock. His torso collapsed against the upward force, and the dynamic suspension of his legs kept him grounded.

Before he could think, Reeves veered, and the tips of his skies left shavings of brown bark sprinkled over the snowy ground. The forest's first scout was the thick stalk of a Blue Spruce, which mauled at the intruder's skis in defense of its territory. Many more followed. Reeves' feet tapped in rapid succession around the battalion of wooden sentries blocking his path.

Time withdrew from the setting, and the steep pitch imposed acute and hazardous speed. The dense foliage left no room to slow down, let alone stop. The luxury of thought was moot, as was any chance to survey the land or pick a line. Reeves had only the immediate choice of life or death. He committed to the speed, having made his choice the moment he got off the chairlift. Nature laid thick tree stoops tighter than any mogul run Reeves ever skied, and the immovable trunks thrusted toward him like a slalom course of bayonets. One slip or false move would leave him mangled in tree bark. He dashed, dodged, and squeezed between the battery of timber. Reeves skiing transformed, not as a matter of survival or even as a means to rescue Godric, but into the legends of a single man in battle against an army. Where the mountain once unwound before Reeves, it now shifted in chaos around him. It no longer heeded his commands; it combatted them. Reeves fought back in kind.

He surrendered his instincts for passivity and defense and attacked the mountain without mercy. His diaphragm constricted, and elbows pressed into his sides, making himself thinner to slip through the narrow crevasses between the trees. He stretched his poles as a speeding marksman, stabbing the snow before each turn. His skis aimed toward the empty spaces, not as if they provided safety but as if they were the exposed flesh of his enemy. Each obstacle he passed set a trap for five more. The mountain forced Reeves into a scurry of snapping turns that kept him ever-pointed along the slope's fall line.

He moved faster in every inch, and with each

surge, the danger grew. The forest continued to dictate his line toward paths incompatible with skiing. His skis cut the veins of exposed roots where the ground refused to hold snow. He plowed through the sagging branches over the only clearings his skis could pass. Reeves punished the forest with each strike. As he skied through the muzzles, the weak branches snapped in half, and others recoiled. Reeves fired through the powdery discharge that exploded as the blows from each tree limb pounded against his unwavering torso.

The whole of his mass centered in his chest—battened by the tight cross studs of muscle squeezing his naval—such that his sternum became an iron bust carried by weightless feet. His boots fused at the ankle, and the base of his skis tapped the snow in a swift rhythm that gave cause for an observer to redefine the term nimble. But the treachery of the forest permitted no witnesses. So often, nature pairs danger with beauty. It is said that God is an artist, and if so, Reeves made every move a photograph worthy of a frame in heaven—should God summon the courage Reeves harbored to capture his image inside Hallow's Gallows.

Escape after escape, the mountain failed to stop Reeves but still forced him on a path of retreat. Just as water takes the path of least resistance, Reeves streamed through the timbered corridors, slipping through the natural channels that the snowmelt would find in the late spring. With each turn, Reeves felt himself straying farther from Godric's footpath. Reaching *The Falls* would be meaningless if he emerged from the tree line alone. Through the forest, Reeves skirted one step ahead of death; to reach Godric, he had to face it head-on. Reeves squeezed his poles as if they were the reigns of the Earth and cut hard against the forest slope.

The forest landscape twisted sideways, flush with trees and no clear path. Reeves made hairpin turns through the tangled hedgerow. With no tangible line, he edged closer to each passing tree. He ducked below the base of a branch too thick to mow down. When he bounced up, his skis caught the stoop of another tree, and his shoulder brushed against its jagged trunk, shredding the fabric of his coat sleeve. Blood pooled over Reeve's burning flesh. Unshaken, he found himself in a thin alleyway that let him gaze ahead, where again he found Godric's tracks crossing the forest.

Reeves lashed a turn back toward the fall line in pursuit of the tracks and the man who left them. He swept around the pivot of a tree stump that knocked the heels of his skis, sending him toward an overhanging tendril between two trunks. Reeves dropped, but the spurs of the branch caught the visor of his helmet, stripping it from his head. His goggles snapped around his neck, and his helmet dangled between his shoulder blades. He lost all bearings, squinting against the rush of icy air collecting in his eyelashes. He peeled toward the brief flashes of light that pulsed through the dark tunnels of his vision. He saw just enough to notice the shadows lifting and a faint glistening of crystals in the snow on the forest floor. Perception precedes knowledge; it showed Reeves that the end of Hallow's Gallows neared. His feet clashed against the side of the slope as his skis dug into the snow, but he still sped downward. With no other option, he collapsed his weight on his uphill arm, which dragged like an anchor against the ground. The staggered base bounced his chest twice until his drag exceeded gravity. Reeves twisted forward to press his chest against the hill. He spread himself wide and grasped the ground with the surface of his body until he laid on his side with the toes of his skis dangling over the cliff above *The Falls*.

Heart and lungs pumped fuel into the chamber of Reeves' idling engine, and the sound of his heaving breath was strong enough to fill the deep gorge of Semitry National Park. Melted snow and hot sweat rippled in a small pool below Reeves's mouth. His body sprawled flat against the precipice. His eyelids fell, and his muscles went limp. Reeves lost all sensation—neither sight, nor sound, nor touch could penetrate his conscious. For a moment, he was a being without context, aware only of himself, and the strength of his own soul filled the void left by an absent universe.

The sight of snow flooded his eyes first. White reflects the full spectrum of light; it was too much for Reeves to bear. The whole of creation followed: the runoff of wet snow dripping around his neck, the burning stretch of his rib cage gasping for air, and the manifest desire for life consuming his aching body. He pressed against the Earth, separating the snow-covered rock from the water made of his own warmth. His sense of touch returned the strength of life to his limbs. Existence pressed his conscious back into his body, which now seemed too small to hold such power, and Reeves released the scream of a life-force, which the world had never before heard, when he realized what he had just done.

The thin snow fell off Reeves as he raised to his feet. His knees locked, and his spine pulled his head and shoulders in a straight line that ran the length of his body, coincident with the cliff. At once, it appeared the the cliff were a podium, and Reeves stood upon it with the same rigid posture he trained himself to hold while skiing, gripping his poles at his hips, and gazing over the valley.

The glory of virtue is promised in death but seldom experienced in life. Reeves' sight fell like a blessing over the landscape, and he saw its reflection. He did not see a forest or snow-capped mountains. He saw an evergreen ocean, flowing with a living tide that rolled in bristled waves and splashed through the valley. And in the distance, crystalline spires broke through the crust of the Earth with a majesty that eclipsed the majestic. They stretched into the fading atmosphere, towards the emerging stars that looked like distant relatives reaching back toward them—both striving to honor the man who cast his gaze upon them.

"If you aren't close to falling, you aren't getting better," a voice called out from the cliffside. "No one can accuse you of being a hypocrite. You are a student of your own teaching."

Reeves stopped, and his eyes followed the voice. He found Godric standing on the precipice, not twenty yards away, stripped of his jacket and shirt, which he had discarded on the ground beside his skis. His muscles rippled under his constricted skin—both in battle against the cold—and revealed the full vitality of youth and strength of the young man.

"You're a fool," Reeves said. "I'm here to teach you. Consider this the final lesson of the day. Get your clothes on. Let's go back."

"I'm no fool. I am enlightened, remember? You admitted so yourself."

"This is not the act of an enlightened man."

"It's the only act I have left."

"That's not true."

"I don't want a sermon, *Brother Reeves*. I'm way past that. You see this?" Godric said, turning his forearm toward Reeves and exposing the tattoo inscribed upon his skin. "It says, '*Woe be the immortal youth, destined to suffer the consequence of age. Bless'd be a young mortality, beknownst only the rapture of life.*' That's what I choose. To know only the rapture of life."

"What does that mean?" Reeves cried.

"I am dying, Zack."

"No man who is dying can do what you did today."

"It's only a matter of time," Godric said behind a gasp of tears. "It's going to take everything. The tremors started over a year ago. Meds can suppress it—for now. Before long, I'll be crippled, a prisoner in my own body. And that's just the start. It's degenerative. Neurons in my brain will rot. I'll come in and out between moments of lucidity and delirium, without the ability to communicate either. I won't be able to walk or read or think. That's my fate. And I say, to hell with that. If fate refutes my will, then I refute fate. I keep my own terms." Godric added with a thin thread of control through broken speech.

"What terms? Life only on the condition of death?"

"It's not death. This world came to life upon my sight. It ends with my last glance upon it."

"Dressing it up with poetics doesn't change anything. However you color it, it's the end of your life."

"But it is beautiful. With my prognosis, this is my best-case scenario. If I die like this, I perish doing what I love on the best day of my life—I have you to thank for that."

"Spare me the gratitude. I'll accept no part in your suicide."

"It's not suicide. There's a chance I make it. You said there's a skiable line. I could find it. I'll be a legend."

"You won't last through the first section. You'll slip off the rock face and die on impact—if you're lucky. Otherwise, you'll freeze. You made certain of that," Reeves said, looking at the orange glow of Godric's coat lying on the snow.

"Damn right. I own my fate."

"Like you said, to hell with fate!" Reeves said, his eyes welling with tears.

"It's my life. My risk to take."

"Skiing *The Falls* is not a risk. It's an out. Living your life is the real risk."

"What would you have me do, Zack? Just wait it out? Go along until the day comes when I can no longer make this choice."

"Yes!" Reeves screamed. "Make every choice up to that point. Stretch the hours of your days as long as possible. Give yourself the chance to live."

"For what?"

"For days like this! And all the ones to come. Stay here and ski every day until your body fails. Or go home. Return to your studies, which you clearly love and have a passion for. Even better: find romance— you're young, fit, intelligent—it will come easier for you than most."

"What like you and Chelle, Zack? I lied. You are a hypocrite. But that doesn't matter. I made my choice way before I met you. You don't get to come into my life for one day and pass judgment like this."

"So don't listen to me. Listen to yourself and your own words. You said yesterday at Steep Easy about what's possible in the near future. 'Imagine,' you said, 'the longest standing questions, answered; the hardest problems, solved; and worst diseases, cured,' your words, Godric, not mine. Breakthroughs will happen! You have to want to see it through."

"No. I refuse to live patiently only to have my patience rewarded with pain. I won't refute the resolve that I hold now in favor of some desperation for a hero to come to my rescue. Like I told Chelle, the hero's place is in fantasy books. Waiting for a hero is to indulge delusions and impossible odds. Miracles don't exist."

Reeves paused and turned toward the marks where he emerged from the dark labyrinth of Hallow's Gallows and the broken snow at the ledge where he stopped. He saw beyond the path that disappeared around the southern bank—he saw the image he captured on video and studied to an eternal memory: the vertical ledge that held but a patchwork of snow in the early spring, that he now envisioned covered after the relentless winter storm.

"What if they do?" Reeves said.

"What the hell are you talking about?"

"What if I show you the impossible made possible?" Reeves said as he clasped his helmet and pulled his goggles over his eyes.

"What are you doing?" Godric spat at Reeves.

"I'm setting the stakes and leaving you with the same choice you left me," Reeves said, digging his poles into the snow and pointing his skis toward the fall line of *The Falls*.

Godric froze. Neither the cold wind splashing against his chest nor the disease lingering deep in his cells could bring him to shiver over the shock of seeing Reeves take mark over *The Falls*. Godric pictured this moment and prepared a rebuttal for every argument against his own descent. He never considered encountering a teacher such as Reeves nor for him to take his place.

"No," Godric wailed. Tears filled his eyes as he watched Reeves prepare to take his place over *The Falls*, considering what Reeves' act would destroy, what it might prove, and how empty the world suddenly seemed if his teacher left it. Godric embraced his world ending; he refused to accept the world persisting without his new teacher.

"Zack, stop. You don't have to do this. I'll pack up right now. We can hike out of here together,"

Godric pleaded to Reeves.

"That won't stop you from returning here tomorrow. Or next week. Or whatever other plan you have to take your own life."

"You don't have to do this for me."

"You're still a fool. I am not doing this for you. You led me here, but I've seen *The Falls* before and walked away. You're right. I am a hypocrite. But that ends today. I dared you to live—that's your risk. This is mine. This is how I have to live."

"You won't make it!" Godric shouted in desperation.

"I will," Reeves said with the same confidence that imparted Godric with freedom in the confines of Offering Bowl. Godric, the disciple, believed his teacher.

Reeves then whispered for the sake of his own ears, "Everything's impossible until it's not."

"What then?" Godric asked, considering a future that he denied for years.

"I'll plant my skis in triumph and march off as the man I wrote about," Reeves said, with a smile as wide as the mountain range that answered the question that Godric never asked, *March where?*

"What about me?" Godric asked aloud.

"My friend, that is up to you," Reeves said his last

words to Godric.

Godric leaned over the edge and watched Reeves drop into the front section of *The Falls*. Reeves' speed was infinite, and he followed a shadowed line with the conviction of a man who believed the last rays of daylight would carry him on a run that would never end. The snow swelled as he dropped, hoisting him in response and presenting Zack Reeves as a master of his art. Godric saw his instructor reach the epitome of his own teaching. As he laid his eyes upon him for the last time, he saw Reeves, not as a skier, nor as a teacher, but as a herald of beauty … of truth … of valor … and more: a hero.

Reeves' line disappeared when he turned over a far corner beyond Godric's sight. Urgency shifted to panic, and he remembered the words of his teacher: "If you have to call for ski patrol, do it immediately. Every passing moment the odds of survival diminish." Godric thought to scream for help, to call on helicopters and rangers to come to Reeves' aid, but Godric remained silent.

He left his life in my hands, Godric thought. No. He made the choice because his life is in his hands. He didn't drop in and tell me to find him or that he'd find me. He dropped for his own good, to manifest his own miracle, to prove it to himself. And in doing so, as an ancillary, he has shown me what good is possible, what can be pursued. His life is not in my hands. But mine is—thanks to him.

Godric lifted his coat out of the muted snow. His body shivered—whether from the cold or his disease did not matter. He would move forward, exercising his will as his teacher did: for days like this; for all those to come; for a hope that in those days, he would again see the impossible made possible.

He read the permanent script on his arm before his slipped it into the sleeve and thought of a new epitaph to be added below it, written in his own tongue:

Woe be the immortal youth; destined to suffer the consequence of age.

Bless'd be a young mortality; beknownst only the rapture of life.

Hallow'd be a herald of beauty, truth, and valor; miracles be thine.

The End.

LUCID FITZPATRICK

ROMANTIC REALIST IN THE 21st CENTURY

Lucid Fitzpatrick is a fiercely independent author. Fans of romanticists, such as Victor Hugo, will immediately recognize and appreciate Lucid Fitzpatrick's style, prose, and characters. Romantic Realism finds a 21st century home in Fitzpatrick's writing as his stories highlight the power of human will, and how personal values drive a character and a story.

"I love to read," Fitzpatrick says. "And it is a pity that I have found far too few books that I loved reading. Those few books have enriched my life in a very profound way. I long for those moments when the author make me want to stand up and shout, 'YES!' to not only the narrative and characters, but to existence and to myself. That is why I choose to write romantic fiction. I see reading as an investment. What I require of my readers is their time and their thought. My goal is to pay back that investment with as many of those 'YES!' moments as I am able to create.

IDEAL READER & IDEALS in WRITING

'My ideal reader seeks affirmation of a prosperous existence and man's noble place within the universe—regardless of circumstance. The underscore of my writing and my brand of romanticism is that affirmation."

Books like *The Fountainhead, Toilers of the Sea,* and *Illusions: The Adventures of a Reluctant Messiah* influenced how Fitzpatrick approaches his plot, characters, setting, and style. The mix of compelling plot, philosophical undertones and overtones, and themes of romanticism make Fitzpatrick's writing unique among contemporary writers, and a much needed voice to an audience hungry for such writing. If you enjoyed reading Hugo, Rand, or Bach, reading the works of Lucid Fitzpatrick will feel like the next step in a natural progression.

Anyone who enjoys these stories is invited follow Lucid Fitzpatrick on social media:

Website: http://lucidfitzpatrick.com
Instagram: https://www.instagram.com/lucididy/
Twitter: https://twitter.com/Lucididy
Facebook: https://www.facebook.com/lucididy1/